365
Stories
and
Rhymes
for
Boys

PRODUCED FOR CHAD VALLEY TOYS
489-499 Avebury Boulevard,
Central Milton Keynes, MK9 2NW

www.argos.co.uk

ISBN 978-1-4723-1092-7
Batch Code: S32328
Made in China

365 Stories and Rhymes for Boys

Contents

The Fox and the Crow

One day, a crow was flying past an open window when she spotted a tasty piece of cheese on the table. There was no one in the room, so she fluttered in and stole the morsel. Then she flew up into the branches of a nearby tree, and was just about to eat it when a fox appeared.

The fox was particularly fond of cheese and he was determined to steal the crow's prize.

"Good morning, Mistress Crow," he greeted her. "May I say that you are looking especially beautiful today? Your feathers are so glossy, and your eyes are as bright as sparkling jewels!"

The fox hoped that the crow would reply and drop the cheese, but she didn't even thank him for his compliments. So he tried again: "You have such a graceful neck, and your claws are really magnificent. They look like the claws of an eagle."

Still the crow ignored him.

The fox could smell the delicious cheese, and it was making his mouth water. He had to find a way to make the crow drop it. At last he came up with a plan.

"All in all, you are a most beautiful bird," he said. "In fact, if your voice matched your beauty, I would call you the Queen of Birds. Why don't you sing a song for me?"

Now, the crow liked the idea of being addressed as the Queen of Birds by all the other creatures in the woods. She thought that the fox would be very impressed by her loud voice, so she lifted her head and started to caw.

Of course, as soon as she opened her beak the piece of cheese fell down, down, down to the ground.

The fox grabbed it in an instant and gobbled it up.

"Thank you," he said. "That was all I wanted. I have to say that you may have a loud voice, but you don't have a very good brain!"

Aesop's moral: Never trust a flatterer.

Pixie Learns to Jump

Pixie watched the other ponies leap over the brook and sighed. She wished she could jump too, but she was afraid.

"You go on," Pixie's mum called to the rest of the herd. "I'll wait for Pixie."

"Okay," called Pixie's big brother. "Last one to the fallen oak is a donkey!"

"Why can't I jump?" wailed Pixie.

"You can," said mum gently. "You just need to learn. Try jumping over that little branch over there."

Pixie looked at the branch, took a deep breath, and rushed at it. **Whoops!** She tripped over and fell flat on her nose.

"You need to slow down," smiled mum, trotting over. "Watch me... Take it steady, don't panic, then glide over."

The next time, Pixie copied her mum and sailed over the branch with ease. She whinnied merrily as she jumped the branch again and again. Then, when she was feeling really brave, she jumped over the brook.

"Last one to the fallen oak is a donkey!" she neighed.

The Singing Dinosaurs

One evening Little Stegosaurus was playing chase in the forest with Diplodocus and Dryosaurus. Suddenly, he stopped and looked around. "Uh-oh!" he said. "I think we're lost."

"And it's getting dark," wailed Dryosaurus.

"Don't panic!" cried Diplodocus in a panicky voice.

"I know," said Little Stegosaurus. "Let's sing. Dad always says that singing makes you feel better!"

The little dinosaurs began to sing their favourite dinosaur hit. **"Doing the dino stomp!"** they roared.

Their singing echoed through the forest and was soon heard by Mr and Mrs Stegosaurus, who were busy searching for the three little dinosaurs. And it wasn't long before it led them to exactly the right place.

"You were right, Dad," laughed Little Stegosaurus, giving his parents a big hug. "Singing does make you feel better – but seeing you and Mum again makes me feel best of all!"

The Donkey and the Load of Salt

One day, a merchant went to collect some sacks of salt from the seashore. He piled the sacks onto the back of his donkey and they started to make their way home.

The donkey struggled to carry the heavy load, and as he crossed a shallow river he slipped on the wet stones. SPLOSH! The sacks tumbled into the water. By the time the man had picked them up, most of the salt had been washed away.

"That's better!" thought the donkey, as the man reloaded the half-empty sacks onto his back. And he trotted on happily down the road.

The following day, the merchant went back to the seashore to get more salt and loaded up the donkey once again.

Now, the donkey was very annoyed at having to carry another heavy load, so when they reached the river on their

way home, he remembered what had happened the day before and pretended to slip. SPLASH! The sacks of salt fell into the water.

By the time the man had hauled them out, the sacks were half empty again, much to the donkey's delight.

The merchant, who was no fool, soon guessed that the donkey had slipped on purpose this time, and he was very angry. So he came up with a plan to teach the lazy creature a lesson.

The next day, he took the donkey to the seashore again, but this time he loaded two large baskets of sponges onto his back. Of course, the sponges were very light, but by the time they reached the river, the rough baskets were beginning to scratch the donkey's shoulders.

"I know, I'll pretend to slip again," thought the crafty creature – and WHOOPS! – he tipped the sponges into the river.

To the donkey's surprise, the merchant did not get angry. He just picked up the sponges and put them back in the baskets.

"Oh, no!" groaned the donkey, as the baskets filled up. The water-soaked sponges were so heavy! He had no choice but to struggle on home, carrying a load ten times heavier than before.

Aesop's moral: One solution does not fit all problems.

Hickory Dickory Dock

Hickory dickory dock,
The mouse ran up the clock.
The clock struck one,
The mouse ran down,
Hickory dickory dock.

Cuckoo, Cherry Tree!

Cuckoo, cherry tree!
Catch a bird and give it to me.
Let the tree be high or low,
Let it hail, rain or snow.

Four-and-twenty Tailors

Four-and-twenty tailors went to catch a snail;
The best man among them
Dared not touch her tail.
She put out her horns like a little Jersey cow.
Run, tailors, run, or she'll catch you all now!

If I Were a Bird

If I were a bird I'd sing a song,
And fly about the whole day long.
And when the night came go to rest,
Up in my cosy little nest.

The Magpie

Magpie, magpie,
Flutter and flee,
Turn up your tail,
And good luck come to me.

Haymaking

The maids in the meadow
Are making the hay,
The ducks in the river
Are swimming away.

Storm Rescue

One windy day there was a big black cloud over the farm. There was a flash of lightning and a loud rumble of thunder.

"Come on, Patch," cried Farmer Fred. "We'll get the animals into the barn."

"Neigh!" said Harry Horse, trying to help. He plodded after Farmer Fred.

"Oh, dear," sighed Harry Horse. "I'm too slow for herding cows and sheep. Perhaps I can help the ducks and hens."

Harry Horse stamped his hoof to nudge the hens towards the barn. But his stamping hooves frightened the hens.

"I'm too big," sighed Harry. "I'm just a useless old horse."

Soon, the animals were safe in the barn. Harry Horse noticed that Polly Pig and her piglets were missing. He neighed and stamped his hoof.

Farmer Fred looked around. "Whizzing hurricanes!" he cried. "Polly and her piglets are missing."

Farmer Fred and the animals raced to Hog Hollow. The storm had blown a tree across the entrance of Polly Pig's sty.

"Polly and her piglets are trapped!" said Farmer Fred. "We'll have to pull that tree out of the way. The tractor won't fit through the gate. But never fear, I've an idea!"

Farmer Fred disappeared into his workshop.

Later, he appeared, grinning. "This," he said, "is the new Mobile Hand-saw. It will cut through the tree in no time!"

Farmer Fred wheeled the Mobile Hand-saw to the pig sty. He flipped a switch and it roared into life. It began to rattle and shake. Then, with a loud *ping* the elastic broke.

"Let's try to lift the tree out of the way," said Farmer Fred.

Farmer Fred and the animals pushed and pulled. But it was no good – the tree wouldn't budge.

"Woof! Woof!" barked Patch, pulling at Harry's old harness.

"Hold on, I've had an idea!" cried Fred. "I know who can help me drag that tree out of the way."

Farmer Fred quickly harnessed Harry Horse. He attached some rope to the harness, and tied the rope around the tree.

"Heave!" cried Farmer Fred. Harry dug in his hooves and heaved. The tree began to slide away from the sty.

At last, Polly and her piglets were free.

"What a useful horse!" cried all the animals.

Harry Horse neighed happily. He was a useful horse, after all!

Bone Crazy

Alfie sat in his basket chewing on a large bone. Mmm! It tasted good.

When he had chewed it for long enough, he took it down to the bottom of the garden, to bury it in his favourite spot beneath the old oak tree. He didn't see next door's dog, Ferdy, watching him through a hole in the fence.

The next day, when Alfie went to dig up his bone, it was gone! He dug all around, but it was nowhere to be found. Then he spied a trail of muddy paw prints leading to the fence, and he guessed what had happened.

Alfie was too big to fit through the fence and get his bone back, so he thought of a plan, instead. Next day he buried another bone. This time, he knew Ferdy was watching him.

Later Alfie hid and watched as Ferdy crept into the garden and started to dig up the bone. Suddenly, Ferdy yelped in pain. The bone had bitten his nose! He flew across the garden and through the fence, leaving the bone behind.

Alfie's friend Mole crept out from where the bone was buried. How the two friends laughed at their trick! And from then on, Ferdy always kept safely to his side of the fence.

One Stormy Night

It was Patch's first night outside in his smart new kennel. He snuggled down on his blanket and watched as dusk fell.

Before long he fell fast asleep. As he slept, big spots of rain began to fall. A splash of water dripped from the kennel roof onto his nose.

Then there was a great crash and a bright flash of light lit up the sky.

Patch woke with a start and was on his feet at once, growling and snarling. "Just a silly storm," he told himself. "Nothing to scare a farm dog!"

But as the lightning flashed yet again, he saw a great shadow looming against the barn. Patch gulped. Whatever could it be? He began to bark furiously, trying to act braver than he felt – and sure enough, next time the lightning flashed, there was no sign of the shadow. "I soon scared that monster away!" he thought.

But as Patch settled back down, the sky outside lit up once more. There in the doorway towered the monster!

"Just checking you're okay in the storm," said Mummy.

"A fearless farm dog like me?" said Patch. "Of course I am!" But as the storm raged on, he snuggled up close to her all the same!

The Hare and the Tortoise

Once upon a time there was a hare who was always boasting about how fast he was.

One day, much to everyone's surprise, after Hare had been boasting even more than normal, Tortoise said, "Okay, Hare. I'll race you."

"Whaaaaat?" laughed Hare. "You've got to be joking." He laughed so much that he fell to his knees and thumped the floor with his fist.

"Tortoise, you're the slowest animal in the forest. I'll run circles around you!" he said.

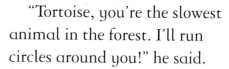

There was a buzz of excitement in the forest the next morning.

"On your marks, get set… *go!*" cried the starting fox.

And Hare flew off at high speed, leaving a cloud of smoke where he had just stood. The tortoise trudged behind much, much, much more slowly.

Hare decided to take a quick look behind to see where the slow tortoise was. When he saw that Tortoise was far, far away, he decided to stop for breakfast. He feasted on some juicy carrots. Then he lay on his back, fiddled with his ears and yawned.

"This is just too easy," he said. "I think I'll have forty winks and catch up with him later." Soon he was fast asleep.

Tortoise plodded on and on. He got to where Hare was lying, fast asleep, and plodded past. He plodded on and on. Hare slept, on and on.

Suddenly Hare awoke with a jolt. He could just see Tortoise in the distance, plodding slowly and carefully towards the finish line.

"Noooooooo!" cried Hare. He leapt to his feet and charged towards the finish as fast as he could. But he was too late. Tortoise was over the line before him. Hare had been beaten.

After that, whenever anyone heard Hare boasting about his speed they reminded him about the day Tortoise beat him.

"Slow and steady won the race," they would say, laughing.

And all Hare could do was smile because, after all, they were quite right.

Little Bo-Peep

Little Bo-Peep has lost her sheep,
And doesn't know where to find them;
Leave them alone,
And they'll come home,
Wagging their tails behind them.

Mary Had a Little Lamb

Mary had a little lamb,
Its fleece was white as snow;
And everywhere that Mary went
The lamb was sure to go.
It followed her to school one day,
Which was against the rule;
It made the children laugh and play
To see a lamb at school.

Baa, Baa, Black Sheep

Baa, baa, black sheep, have you any wool?
Yes sir, yes sir, three bags full.
One for the master,
And one for the dame,
And one for the little boy
Who lives down the lane.

Here's the Lady's Knives and Forks

Here's the lady's knives and forks.
Here's the lady's table.
Here's the lady's looking glass.
And here's the baby's cradle.
Rock! Rock! Rock! Rock!

On Oath

As I went to Bonner,
I met a pig
Without a wig,
Upon my word and honour.

Bless You

Bless you, bless you, burnie-bee,
Tell me when my wedding be;
If it be tomorrow day,
Take your wings and fly away.
Fly to the east, fly to the west,
Fly to him I love the best.

The Vain Crow

Once upon a time, a crow was flying far from home when he saw a pair of peacocks in a beautiful garden. The crow had never seen such colourful feathers, so he flew down and asked the pair what kind of birds they were.

"We're peacocks," they said proudly, and strutted up and down displaying their magnificent tails.

The crow flew away feeling ashamed of his dull, black feathers. Every time he caught sight of his reflection, he remembered the peacocks and their fabulous blue-green plumage. How he wished he looked like them!

One day the crow spotted a familiar-looking feather on the ground. It must have fallen from a peacock's tail. The crow picked it up and took it back to his nest. The next day he returned to the same place and found another feather. Day after day, the crow went back until he had collected seven fabulous tail feathers.

The crow stuck the peacock feathers
to his own black tail and strutted
back and forth in front of the other
crows, waiting for them to admire
him, just as he had admired the
peacocks. But instead of being
impressed, the other crows just
laughed at him and told him
he looked ridiculous.

"I don't care. I don't belong with you
boring black crows," the vain crow told the rest of the flock.
"I'm going to join the peacocks in their beautiful garden."

So the crow flew back to the garden and landed among the
peacocks and peahens. He was sure they would welcome him,
but the peacocks and peahens knew right away that he was
an impostor.

"You're not one of us!" they called. Then they
plucked out his borrowed feathers and started to peck him
until he had no choice but to fly back home.

At last the crow realised there was no point in pretending
to be something that he was not, and he was looking forward
to getting back home. But when he rejoined the other crows,
they drove him away. "You're not one of us!" they cawed.

So the vain crow flew away sadly, alone, and all because he
was not satisfied with his appearance.

Aesop's moral: Be happy with who you are.

The Fox and Grapes

One summer day, a fox was walking through a field when he saw a bunch of juicy grapes dangling high above his head.

"I wish I could have some of those to quench my thirst," he said to himself – but the grapes were out of reach.

The fox stood on his back legs and stretched his neck as far as he could, but the grapes were still too high up. He took several steps backwards, ran towards the grapevine and took a giant leap… but he missed them!

So the fox tried again from the other direction. He ran as fast as he could and sprang into the air… but he missed them once more. Determined to get the delicious grapes, the fox jumped again and again and again. Now he was even hotter and thirstier than before – and he still hadn't managed to reach a single grape!

Finally, the fox looked at the grapes with disgust.

"I don't know why I'm wasting my time trying to get those horrible grapes," he said. "I'm sure they taste really sour!"

Aesop's moral: If someone can't get something, they pretend it is not worth having.

Dog and His Reflection

One day, a hungry dog was passing a butcher shop when he spotted a juicy steak lying on the counter. The dog's mouth watered at the sight, so he waited until the butcher went out to the back of the shop, then he ran in and stole it.

On his way home, the dog crossed a narrow bridge over a river. As he looked down into the water he saw another dog looking up at him. This dog was also carrying a piece of meat, and it looked even bigger than the one he already had!

"I want that one!" thought the greedy dog, so he dropped his own steak into the water and jumped into the river to steal it.

But as he reached out to snatch the prize in his jaws, the steak disappeared, and the greedy dog's jaws bit on nothing more than water. He had been fooled by his own reflection – and was left with nothing to eat at all!

Aesop's moral: It doesn't pay to be greedy.

Why Owls Stare

Once upon a time there lived an owl and a pigeon.
They were friends, but they were great rivals too,
and they were always boasting to one another.

"Owls have much better eyesight than pigeons," the owl
would claim.

"Pigeons are much better at flying," the pigeon would reply.

"Owls have better hearing," the owl would brag.

"Pigeons have prettier feathers," the pigeon would argue.

One morning they were sitting side by side on a branch when
the owl said, "I think there are many more owls than pigeons."

"That can't be right," replied the pigeon. "There are
definitely far more pigeons than owls. There's only one way to
find out. I challenge you to count them!"

"All right," the owl agreed. "We will need a place with plenty
of trees. Let's do it in the Big Wood a week from today. That
will give us time to let everyone know."

During that week the owl and the pigeon flew in
every direction to tell their fellow birds to come to the
Big Wood to be counted.

The day of the count came, and the owls were the first
to arrive. It seemed as if every tree was full
of owls hooting at each other.

There were so many, the owls were sure they would outnumber the pigeons.

Suddenly the sky went dark. Clouds of pigeons were flying towards the Big Wood. They came from the north, the south, the east and the west. Soon there was no space left in the trees, and branches were starting to break under the weight of all the pigeons.

More and more pigeons came, circling above the wood, looking for a place to land. By now, the ground was completely covered with pigeons, too. The owls were wide-eyed with amazement as they stared at all the pigeons, who were still arriving by their thousands. The noise of their wings was deafening, and the owls were getting squashed and trampled by the ones who had managed to find a perch in the trees.

"Let's get out of here," the owls hooted to one another, flying away. But the poor creatures had stared so long and hard at the pigeons that their eyes stayed stuck wide open – and from that day on owls always stared, and hid during the day when the pigeons were nearby, flying only at night.

See-saw, Sacradown

See-saw, Sacradown,
Which is the way to London Town?
One foot up and one foot down,
That's the way to London Town.

Over the Hills and Far Away

When I was young and had no sense,
I bought a fiddle for eighteen pence,
And the only tune that I could play
Was, 'Over the Hills and Far Away'.

As I Was Going Along

As I was going along, long, long,
A-singing a comical song, song, song,
The lane that I went on was so long, long, long,
And the song that I sang was as long, long, long,
And so I went singing along.

A Sailor Went to Sea

A sailor went to sea, sea, sea,
To see what he could see, see, see,
But all that he could see, see, see,
Was the bottom of the deep blue sea, sea, sea.

The Grand Old Duke of York

The grand old Duke of York,
He had ten thousand men;
He marched them up to the top of the hill,
And he marched them down again!

And when they were up they were up,
And when they were down they were down;
And when they were only halfway up,
They were neither up nor down.

What Is the Rhyme for Porringer?

What is the rhyme for porringer?
The King he had a daughter fair,
And gave the Prince of Orange her.

Go to Bed

Go to bed late,
Stay very small;
Go to bed early
Grow very tall.

Lionel Can Sing!

Lionel was a happy elephant and always singing – but his singing didn't make everyone else happy. It was much too noisy!

"Be quiet!" his friends would roar, every time he sang.

One day, after his friends had yelled back, **"Be quiet!"** particularly loudly, Lionel started to feel really sad.

"What you need is singing lessons," said his friend Mouse. "Let's ask Bluebird."

So Lionel lifted Mouse onto his back and together they went to Bluebird's tree in the jungle.

When Lionel explained the problem, Bluebird was happy to help.

"Breathe in deeply," she told him. "Let your chest fill with air, then blow out through your trunk s...l...o...w...l...y!"

It wasn't long before Lionel was singing as sweetly as a bluebird – but a little more loudly. "I can sing after all," cried Lionel happily. **"TOOTLE! TOOT!"**

Practice Makes Perfect

One day a sign appeared on the monkey puzzle tree.

"Acrobatic competition at Treetop School this Friday," read Ralph the monkey. "All welcome."

Ralph chattered excitedly. He loved acrobatics.

"I'm going to enter," he informed his mum. "I'll have to practise hard." Then he leaped into the air and did a cartwheel.

"Please do be careful," cried Mum.

But Ralph wasn't listening. He bounced higher and higher, until – ouch! – he landed on his head with a thump.

"Oooo!" groaned Ralph. "I don't think I want to do acrobatics any more."

"Why don't you practise on your bed," suggested Mum. "That way, it won't hurt if you fall."

"What a good idea," cried Ralph.

After that, Ralph practised his tricks every night in his bedroom – rolly-polies, high jumps, handstands and even cartwheels. By the day of the competition, Ralph was able to do them all perfectly. And guess who won the competition? Ralph, of course.

"Practice makes perfect!" grinned Ralph, holding up his trophy.

What's That Noise?

Little Cub lived on the grassy plain with his mum and sister Tia. Little Cub loved playing with his mum and Tia, but sometimes he enjoyed wandering off on his own.

   One day Little Cub decided to explore a new part of the plain. He prowled through the grass, admiring the acacia trees and saying hello to everyone who crossed his path.

He was busy introducing himself to a pretty butterfly, when he heard a loud **grunt**, followed by a big SPLASH! Something was making lots of noise nearby.

   Little Cub jumped with fright. "Ooooh," he wailed. "W…w…what was that?" He was so scared that he buried his head beneath his paws and tried to hide.

Then a horrible, haunting hoooowl filled the air. Little Cub covered his ears and quaked with fear. He had never heard anything quite so strange. "Maybe it's a scary, lion-eating monster," he worried.

Just then, Giraffe came ambling through the grass, and he was heading straight for the terrible noise. Little Cub tried to wave to him, but it was no use. Giraffe just kept on going. Suddenly, Little Cub remembered that he was a brave lion. He wasn't scared of anything.

"Wait," he roared bravely. "Let me go first and find out what's making that awful noise."

Giraffe looked surprised – but he let Little Cub lead the way. Little Cub poked his head through the grass, ready to pounce on whatever danger lay ahead.

But he didn't pounce. He didn't even roar. Instead, he began to laugh. It wasn't a scary, lion-eating monster, after all. Can you guess? It was Harold the Hippo singing in the bath!

Merry's Big Wish

Once upon a time there was
a beautiful wooden horse named
Merry who lived on a merry-go-
round on the end of a seaside
pier. But Merry wasn't just an
ordinary wooden horse. He was
very special! Every day people
would come along to pat his

nose and make a wish. And almost always that wish would
come true. For you see, Merry was said to have come from a
magical land far away.

Merry loved giving rides to all the little children, and he loved
making wishes come true. But Merry had a wish of his own.
He wished he were real, so that he could gallop across the soft
sand and splash through gentle waves on the seashore.

One night, when everyone had gone home for the day, Merry
heard a neigh and a beautiful white mare appeared.

"Come with me," called the mare.

"I can't," replied Merry.
"I'm not real."

"Anything is
possible," said the
mare, blowing
softly on Merry's
well-rubbed nose.

Suddenly a strange feeling came over Merry. His nose began to tingle and his legs began to twitch. Then he kicked his legs into the air and he was free. He raced after the white mare and splashed through the waves.

"Neigghhh!" cried Merry, as he and the white mare galloped on and on through the night. They didn't stop until they came to a faraway land full of snowy white horses.

"Where are we?" asked Merry.

"This is your home," replied the white mare. "The land where you came from. And all these horses are your brothers and sisters. From now on you will live here with us."

"But what about the merry-go-round and all the little children? And what about the wishes?"

"Don't worry," replied the white mare. "You can work on the merry-go-round each day, then return home each night."

"Neigghhh!" squealed Merry, tossing his mane into the air. "Now I am the happiest horse in the world."

How the Kangaroo Got His Tail

Once upon a time, a kangaroo and a wombat lived together in a hut. Back then, kangaroos had no tails and wombats had round heads, so they looked different from the way they do today. Although they enjoyed each other's company, the kangaroo liked to sleep outside and the wombat preferred to sleep indoors.

"Why don't you come and sleep outside with me?" the kangaroo would say. "It's lovely to look at the stars and listen to the sound of the wind in the trees."

"It's too cold and it might rain," the wombat would reply. "I'd much rather sleep in the hut in front of the fire."

As winter approached, the wind became stronger and colder.

"I don't mind a bit of wind," the kangaroo told himself as he huddled up next to a tree, trying to keep warm. Then it began

to rain. By the middle of the night the kangaroo felt so frozen, he pushed open the door to the hut and went inside.

"You'll have to sleep in the corner," muttered the sleepy wombat, who was snoozing by the fire. "I don't want you making me all wet."

So the poor kangaroo curled up in the draughty corner, where the rain blew in through a hole in the wall.

In the morning, the kangaroo was cold and grumpy.

"Wake up, you selfish wombat!" he yelled.

The wombat awoke with a start, then tripped and banged his head on the floor, flattening his forehead.

The kangaroo laughed. "That's what you get for not letting me get warm by the fire. Your flat forehead will be a reminder of how badly you treated me last night!"

The wombat was so angry, he picked up a stick and threw it. The stick bounced off the wall and hit the kangaroo, sticking in his bottom.

"And from now on that will be your tail!" laughed the wombat. "It serves you right!"

And THAT is why wombats have flat foreheads, and kangaroos have long tails.

Chalk and Cheese

Chalk and Cheese were as different as two kittens can be. Chalk was fluffy and white. She liked dishes of cream and lazing in the sun. Cheese was a rough, tough black kitten. He liked chewing on fish bones and climbing trees. Their mother puzzled over her odd little kittens, but she loved them both the same.

One day, Cheese climbed high up on the barn and got stuck. "Help!" he cried to his sister.

"I don't like climbing!" she said, opening one eye.

"If only you were like me," said Cheese, "you could help!"

"If only you were like me," said Chalk, "you wouldn't have got stuck!" And with that she went back to sleep.

Just then, the farm dog came by. Chalk sprang up as he gave a loud bark and began to chase her.

"Help!" she cried to Cheese, up on the barn.

"I'm stuck, remember?" he cried. "You shouldn't lie where dogs can chase you."

Then Mummy appeared. She swiped the dog away with her claws, then climbed up and rescued Cheese.

"If only you were both more like me," she said, "you'd keep out of danger and look after each other."

And from then on, that's just what they did.

Oscar the Octopus

Oscar the Octopus was a keen footballer. With his many feet he was a real menace to the other team.

Oscar began to get ready for today's big match. He stretched out a tentacle and put on the first boot, then he put on the second. As Oscar put on boot three the crowds had begun to gather beside the sea to watch the match. He could hear them singing football songs.

On went boot five as the crowd swayed and cheered loudly. The harder Oscar tried to hurry, the longer it seemed to take!

Boot number six went on, and Oscar stood on his head and practised some tricks, then boot seven – he was almost ready. Now it was the last one – boot eight. Oscar was getting nervous and the laces were so fiddly that it took him ages.

At last he was ready and on to the pitch he went.

But the referee said, "Sorry, Oscar! You're too late. The game is over, the whistle has blown. Nobody scored and the crowd has gone home!"

Tom, He Was a Piper's Son

Tom, he was a piper's son,
He learnt to play when he was young,
And the only tune that he could play,
Was, 'Over the hills and far away'.
Over the hills and a great way off,
The wind shall blow my topknot off!

The Squirrel

The winds they did blow,
The leaves they did wag;
Along came a beggar boy,
And put me in his bag.

He took me to London,
A lady me did buy,
Put me in a silver cage,
And hung me up on high.

With apples by the fire,
And nuts for me to crack,
Besides a little feather bed
To rest my little back.

Go to Bed, Tom

Go to bed, Tom, go to bed, Tom,
Tired or not, Tom, go to bed, Tom.

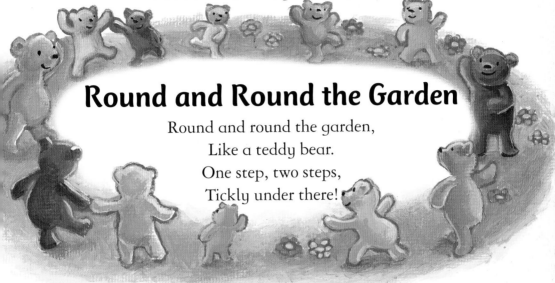

Round and Round the Garden

Round and round the garden,
Like a teddy bear.
One step, two steps,
Tickly under there!

Charley Warley

Charley Warley had a cow,
Black and white about the brow;
Open the gate and let her through,
Charley Warley's old cow.

Daddy

Bring Daddy home with a fiddle and a drum,
A pocket full of spices, an apple and a plum.

Clumsy Fred

Clumsy Fred seemed to be a very cross and very clumsy giant! He bumped into castles and turned homes into rubble. He sent garden sheds flying as he strode across the town, and he trod on lamp posts, demolishing them.

The townspeople were very concerned. What was the matter with Fred? He didn't use to be so cross and clumsy. There was definitely something wrong, but no one was sure how to help.

Then a monster expert came to the rescue. He went to see Fred in his cave above the town.

Fred was feeling very sorry for himself. "Why am I so clumsy?" he asked. "I don't like upsetting everyone, but I just can't help it!"

The expert did a lot of tests. Finally he found the solution. "I know what is wrong!" he said. "The problem is your eye. You're short-sighted!"

The expert gave Fred a monocle to try out. "I can see!" he cried.

And that was the end of Clumsy Fred!

Not Another Bear

Tyler loved teddy bears. When asked what he would like for his birthday, or Christmas, Tyler's answer was always the same: "A teddy bear, please!"

"Not another bear!" his parents would say. "Look at your bed, Tyler. There's no room for any more!"

It was true. There were bears all over Tyler's bed. Every night Tyler had to squeeze into the tiny space that was left. But Tyler didn't mind at all.

"We've got to do something about this," said Tyler's dad one day, marching into Tyler's bedroom with a pile of wood and a bag of tools. By tea time there were three shelves on Tyler's bedroom wall, and a row of bears sat neatly on each one.

Next day was the school fair. As they walked in, Mum gave Tyler some pocket money. "Find something you'd like to buy," she said.

"What did you buy, Tyler?" Mum asked, when they got home. Tyler grinned.

"Not another bear!" sighed Mum.

"But there's plenty of room now," Tyler answered. He winked at the new bear. And Tyler was sure that the bear winked back!

If You Hold My Hand

Oakey's mum opened the front door. "Come on, Oakey. Let's go outside and explore."

But Oakey wasn't really sure. He was only small, and the world looked big and scary.

"Only if you promise to hold my hand," said Oakey.

"This looks like a great place to play. Shall we take a look? What do you say?" asked Oakey's mum.

"Only if you promise to hold my hand," said Oakey. And Oakey did it!

"This slide looks like fun. Would you like to try?" asked Oakey's mum.

"I'm only small," said Oakey. "I don't know if I can climb that high – unless you hold my hand."

And Oakey did it! "*Wheee!* Did you see me?" he cried.

"We'll take a short cut through the woods," said Oakey's mum.

"I'm not sure if we should," said Oakey. "It looks dark in there. Well, I suppose we could – will you hold my hand?"

And Oakey did it! "*Boo!* I scared you!" he cried.

Deep in the woods, Oakey found a stream, shaded by beautiful tall trees.

"Stepping stones, look!" said Oakey's mum. "Do you think you could jump across these?"

"Maybe," said Oakey. "I just need you to hold my hand, please."

And Oakey did it!

Beyond the woods, Oakey and his mum ran up the hill, and all the way down to the sea.

"Come on, Oakey," called his mum. "Would you like to paddle in the sea with me?" But the sea looked big, and he was only small.

Suddenly, Oakey knew that didn't matter at all.

He turned to his mum and smiled… "I can do anything if you hold my hand," he said.

The Three Billy Goats Gruff

Once upon a time there were three Billy Goats Gruff. There was a big goat, a middle-sized goat and a little goat.

The three goats all loved to eat grass. They ate grass all day long on the hill. But they never crossed the bridge to eat the grass on the other side, because a troll lived under the bridge.

One day the little Billy Goat Gruff looked at the green grass on the other side of the bridge. "I'm not scared of a silly old troll," he said. "I'm going to cross the bridge."

So the little Billy Goat Gruff set off across the bridge.

Trip, trap, trip, trap went his hooves.

"Who's that trip-trapping over my bridge?" roared the troll.

"It's only me!" said the little Billy Goat Gruff. "I'm going to eat the green grass on the other side of the bridge."

"Oh no, you're not!" roared the troll. "I'm going to eat you up!"

"But I'm just little," said the little Billy Goat Gruff. "Wait until the middle-sized goat comes across."

So the little Billy Goat Gruff crossed the bridge.

Next, the middle-sized Billy Goat Gruff crossed the bridge.

"Who's that trip-trapping over my bridge?" roared the troll.

"It's only me!" said the middle-sized Billy Goat Gruff. "I'm going to eat the green grass on the other side of the bridge."

"Oh no, you're not!" roared the troll. "I'm going to eat you up!"

"But I'm just middle-sized," said the middle-sized Billy Goat Gruff. "Wait until the big goat comes across."

So the middle-sized Billy Goat Gruff crossed the bridge.

Next the big Billy Goat Gruff crossed the bridge.

"Who's that trip-trapping over my bridge?" roared the troll.

"It's only me!" said the big Billy Goat Gruff. "I'm going to eat the green grass on the other side of the bridge."

"Oh no, you're not!" roared the troll. "I'm going to eat you up!"

The troll jumped onto the bridge. The big Billy Goat Gruff lowered his horns.

Crash! Splash! The troll fell into the water.

The big Billy Goat Gruff skipped over the bridge and soon he was eating the green grass with the other Billy Goats Gruff.

And the bad troll was never seen again.

The Hermit Crab

The hermit crab's a nervous chap,
He wears his home upon his back,
He's often shy, and likes to hide.
If he's scared, he pops inside.
Two beady eyes look all about,
And when it's safe he creeps back out.

Five Teddy Bears

Five teddy bears came out one night,
To dance beneath the pale moonlight,
And count the stars above their head,
(When little bears should be in bed),
Until the sun came up, and then ...
The naughty bears crept home again.

Three Grey Geese

Three grey geese
In a green field grazing,
Grey were the geese
And green was the grazing.

Grey were the geese,
Green was the grazing,
That's my tale.
Isn't that amazing!

(Repeat the rhyme as fast as you can.)

A Nutty Adventure

Paddy the squirrel was busy scurrying around the forest floor, gathering nuts for his winter store. Then, when he was sure nobody was looking, he pushed each one into his secret hidey-hole in the Giant Beech.

It was hard work, and by noon Paddy decided to take a break. He crept back to the Giant Beech and peeped into the hole to see how many nuts he had collected. You can imagine his horror when he saw that the hidey-hole was empty. All the nuts were gone!

"Someone's stolen my hoard," he shouted angrily. He was so loud, his friends came out to see what was wrong.

"You think that's bad," cried Rabbit, who was rubbing his head. "Someone has been dropping nuts on my head. I've just had to sweep a whole heap out of my door."

Suddenly Badger began to laugh. He knew exactly what had happened. Paddy had been putting his nuts through Rabbit's window!

When Badger explained, Paddy and Rabbit began to chuckle.

"What a nutty adventure," said Paddy.

The Open Road

"Ratty," said Mole, one bright summer morning, "I want to ask you a favour."

"Why, certainly," said Ratty, who was sitting by the river.

"Well, what I wanted to ask you is, can we call on Mr Toad? I've heard so much about him."

"Get the boat out and we'll paddle up there at once. Toad is always in and will be delighted to meet you."

Rat and Mole rounded a bend in the river and came in sight of a handsome old stone house.

"There's Toad Hall," said Ratty. "It is the biggest house in these parts."

They moored the boat on the bank and started to walk towards Toad Hall.

"Hooray!" cried Toad as the three animals shook paws.

"The very fellows I wanted to see! You've got to help me sort out something really important!"

"It's about boating, I suppose?" asked the Rat.

"Forget about that!" cried the Toad. "I gave that up ages ago.

Now I've discovered the **real** thing. Come with me!"

He led the way to the stable yard, where, in the open, was a shiny new gypsy caravan with red wheels.

"There!" cried Toad. "There's the **real** life. A home away from home, travelling the road without a care in the world."

Mole followed Toad up the steps and inside. Ratty remained where he was, hands thrust deep in his pockets.

"I've thought of everything," cried Toad. He pulled open a cupboard. "Here's everything we could possibly want to eat."

He threw open another cupboard. "Here's all the clothes we need! We must start at once."

"I beg your pardon," said Rat, "but did I hear you say *we?*"

"Now, dear Ratty," said Toad calmly, "don't get on your high horse. You've got to come."

"I'm not coming, and that is that," said the Rat.

"Me neither," said Mole, siding loyally with Ratty.

"All the same…" he added, "it does sound like fun."

"I'll say it would be fun," said Toad, and he began to paint the joys of caravanning. In no time at all, even Rat was interested.

And so it was that all three friends set off that afternoon to discover the joys of caravanning on the open road.

"This is the life, eh!" said a sleepy Toad that evening, when they stopped for supper. "Better than talking about your river, eh, Ratty?"

"I don't talk about my river, Toad," replied Rat. "You know I don't. But I think about it," he added quietly, "all the time."

Mole reached out and squeezed Ratty's paw. "Dear Ratty," he whispered. "Should we run away tomorrow and go back to our dear old hole on the river?"

"No, we'll see it out," whispered the Rat. "We must stick by Toad until he's over this craze. It won't take long."

The end was nearer than even Rat suspected. Next morning, Mole turned the horse's head onto their first really wide main road. In the distance they heard a faint warning hum, like the buzz of a bee. An instant later, with a loud BEEP!, a whirl of wind, and a blast of sound, a motor car tore past.

The old horse who was pulling the caravan let out a whinny of fear, reared, then plunged and bucked, driving the caravan into a ditch, where it landed with a huge crash.

Ratty danced with rage. "You villains!" he shouted, shaking both fists. "You scoundrels, you … you … road hogs!"

Mole looked down at the caravan. Panels and windows were smashed, the axles hopelessly bent, and cans of food were scattered about. And Toad? Toad sat in the middle of the road staring in the direction of the now disappeared car.

Rat shook him by the shoulder. "Come on, Toad, do get up!"

But Toad wouldn't move. "Glorious!" he murmured. "That's the way to travel. Oh, bliss! Oh, beep beep!"

"Oh, drat Toad!" said Ratty crossly. "I'm done with him! I've seen it all before. He's off onto a new craze. He'll be in a dream for days. We'll just have to get him to his feet, then make our way to the nearest town and catch a train home."

"Now, look here, Toad!" said Ratty. "You'll have to make a complaint against that scoundrel and his car.

"Me? Complain?" murmured Toad. "I wouldn't dream of it. I'm going to order one right away!"

Ratty sighed. Some things would never change.

Birds of a Feather

Birds of a feather flock together.
And so will pigs and swine.
Rats and mice will have their choice,
And so will I have mine.

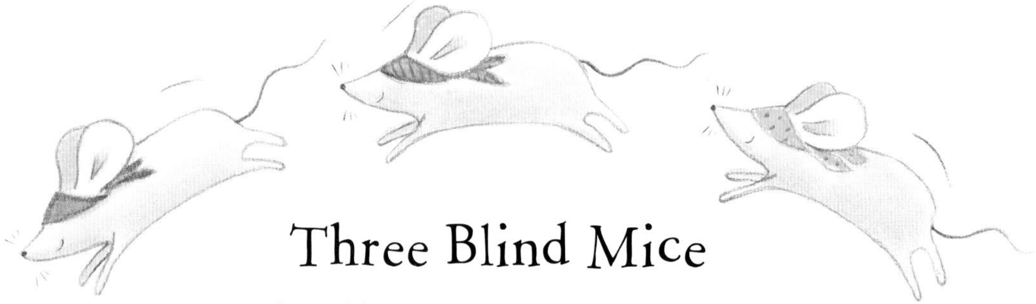

Three Blind Mice

Three blind mice, three blind mice,
See how they run, see how they run!
They all ran after the farmer's wife,
Who cut off their tails with a carving knife.
Did you ever see such a thing in your life
As three blind mice?

Down With the Lambs

Down with the lambs,
Up with the lark,
Run to bed children,
Before it gets dark.

Brown Owl

The Brown Owl sits in the ivy-bush,
And she looketh wondrous wise,
With a horny beak beneath her cowl,
And a pair of large round eyes.

Dandy

I had a dog and his name was Dandy,
His tail was long and his legs were bandy,
His eyes were brown and his coat was sandy,
The best in the world was my dog Dandy.

Little Miss Muffet

Little Miss Muffet
Sat on a tuffet,
Eating her curds and whey.
Along came a spider,
Who sat down beside her
And frightened Miss Muffet away.

Billy Fox Is Bored

Billy looked out of the kitchen window and sighed. It was so cold and windy that he couldn't go out to play.

He had played with all of his toys. He had finished his favourite book. He had tidied up his bedroom, and had even straightened out his sock drawer. Now there was nothing left to do but peer out of the window and watch the leaves blow by.

"I'm bored," he sighed. "There's nothing to do. Can't I go outside?"

"No," replied Dad gently. "There's a big storm on its way and I don't want you to get caught in it. Why don't we just spend a little time together?'

"But staying inside is boring," moaned Billy Fox. "I want to go out and play with my friends."

"I'm afraid you can't," Dad said firmly. "Do you want to help me make cakes instead? They're your favourite – Woodland Crunch."

"I suppose so," muttered Billy, not sounding at all interested. He watched his dad pour the ingredients into a bowl and sighed wearily.

"Come on," smiled Dad. "Help me mix it all together."

He passed Billy a wooden spoon and soon they were both stirring the bowl energetically.

"**Brrrrrrr!**" went Dad, pretending to be a cement mixer.

"**Brrrrrrr!**" Billy joined in. And soon Billy actually found that, much to his surprise, he was enjoying himself.

Before long, the cakes were ready to go into the hot oven.

"Now we just have to wait for them to cook," said Dad.

"But that's ages!" said Billy.

"Sit back and I'll tell you a story while we wait," suggested Dad. "Once upon a time…"

Dad finished the story just as the cakes came out of the oven. Before long Billy was munching one.

"That was good," cried Billy, licking his lips. "But not as good as spending time with you, Dad. Can we do it again tomorrow?"

Three Young Rats

Three young rats with black felt hats,
Three young ducks with white straw flats,
Three young dogs with curling tails,
Three young cats with demi-veils,
Went out to walk with two young pigs
In satin vests and sorrel wigs;
But suddenly it chanced to rain,
And so they all went home again.

Humpty Dumpty

Humpty Dumpty sat on a wall,
Humpty Dumpty had a great fall;
All the king's horses and all the king's men
Couldn't put Humpty together again.

We're All in the Dumps

We're all in the dumps,
For diamonds and trumps,
The kittens are gone to St Paul's,
The babies are bit,
The moon's in a fit,
And the houses are built without walls.

Tweedle-dum and Tweedle-dee

Tweedle-dum and Tweedle-dee
Agreed to have a battle,
For Tweedle-dum said Tweedle-dee
Had spoiled his nice new rattle.
Just then flew down a monstrous crow,
As big as a tar-barrel,
Which frightened both the heroes so,
They quite forgot their quarrel.

Daffy-Down-Dilly

Daffy-Down-Dilly
Has come up to town
In a yellow petticoat
And a green gown.

Little Tommy Tittlemouse

Little Tommy Tittlemouse
Lived in a little house;
He caught fishes
In other men's ditches.

The Velveteen Rabbit

Once upon a time, there was a
Velveteen Rabbit made from soft
fur, with ears lined with pink
satin. When he was given
to the Boy on Christmas
morning, he was the best
present.

At first, the Boy thought the
Velveteen Rabbit was wonderful,
but then he put him away in the
cupboard.

"What is real?" the Velveteen Rabbit asked the toys in the
cupboard one day.

"It's what you become when a child really loves you,"
explained a hobbyhorse. "I was made real a long time ago
by the Boy's uncle. It can take a very long time. By the time
you are real some of your fur has dropped out. But it doesn't
matter, because once you are real you can't be ugly."

One night, when Nanny was putting the Boy to bed
she couldn't find his favourite toy. So she grabbed the Velveteen
Rabbit by his ear.

"Here, take your old bunny!" she said. And from that night
on, the Velveteen Rabbit slept with the Boy.

At first it was a bit uncomfortable. The Boy would hug him

so tightly that the Velveteen Rabbit could hardly breathe. But soon he grew to love sleeping with the Boy. And when the Boy went to sleep, the Rabbit would snuggle down and dream about becoming real.

The Velveteen Rabbit went wherever the Boy went. He had rides in the wheelbarrow, and picnics on the grass. He was so happy that he didn't notice that his fur was getting shabby.

One day, the Boy left the Rabbit on the lawn. At bedtime, Nanny came to fetch the Rabbit because the Boy couldn't go to sleep without him.

"Imagine all that fuss about a toy," said Nanny.

"He isn't a toy. He's real!" cried the Boy.

When the Rabbit heard these words he was filled with joy! He was real! The Boy himself had said so.

Late one afternoon, the Boy left the Rabbit in the woods while he went to pick some flowers. Suddenly, two strange creatures appeared. They looked like the Velveteen Rabbit, but they were very fluffy. They were wild rabbits.

"Why don't you come and play with us?" one of them asked.

"I don't want to," said the Velveteen Rabbit. He didn't want to tell them that he couldn't move. But all the time he was longing to dance like them.

One of the wild rabbits danced

so close to the Velveteen Rabbit that it brushed against his ear. Then he wrinkled up his nose and jumped backwards.

"He doesn't smell right," the wild rabbit cried. "He isn't a rabbit at all! He isn't **real!"**

"I am real," said the Velveteen Rabbit. "The Boy said so."

Just then, the Boy ran past and the wild rabbits disappeared.

"Come back and play!" called the Velveteen Rabbit. But there was no answer. Finally, the Boy took him home.

A few days later, the Boy fell ill. Nanny and a doctor fussed around his bed. No one took any notice of the Velveteen Rabbit snuggled beneath the blankets.

Then, little by little, the Boy got better. The Rabbit listened to Nanny and the doctor talk. They were going to take the Boy to the seaside.

"Hurrah!" thought the Rabbit, who couldn't wait to go, too.

But the Velveteen Rabbit was put into a sack and carried to the bottom of the garden, ready to be put on the bonfire.

That night, the Boy slept with a new toy for company. Meanwhile, at the bottom of the garden, the Velveteen Rabbit was feeling lonely and cold. He wiggled until his head poked out of the sack and looked around. He remembered all the fun he had with the Boy. He thought about the wise hobbyhorse.

He wondered what use it was being loved and becoming real if he ended up alone. A real tear trickled down his velvet cheek onto the ground.

Then a strange thing happened. A tiny flower sprouted out of the ground. The petals opened, and out flew a tiny fairy.

"Little Rabbit," she said, "I am the Nursery Fairy. When toys are old and worn and children don't need them anymore, I take them away and make them real."

"Wasn't I real before?" asked the Rabbit.

"You were **real** to the Boy," the Fairy said, "But now you shall be **real** to everyone."

The Fairy caught hold of the Velveteen Rabbit and flew with him into the woods where the wild rabbits were playing.

"I've brought you a new playmate," said the Fairy. And she put the Velveteen Rabbit down on the grass.

The little rabbit didn't know what to do. Then something tickled his face and, before he knew what he was doing, he lifted his leg to scratch his nose. He could move! The little rabbit jumped into the air with joy. He was **real** at last.

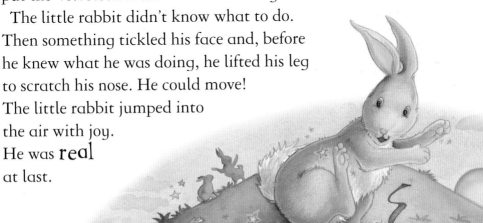

Brown Bird

Little brown bird,
Where do you live?
"Up on yonder wood, sir,
On a hazel twig."

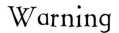

Warning

The robin and the redbreast,
The robin and the wren:
If you take them from their nest
You'll never thrive again.

Cock Crow

The cock's on the woodpile
Blowing his horn,
The bull's in the barn
A-threshing the corn.

Cats and Dogs

Hoddley, poddley, puddle and fogs,
Cats are to marry the poodle dogs;
Cats in blue jackets and dogs in red hats,
What will become of the mice and the rats?

Feathers

Cackle, cackle, Mother Goose,
Have you any feathers loose?
"Truly have I, pretty fellow,
Half enough to fill a pillow.
Here are quills, take one or two,
And down to make a bed for you."

Fishes Swim

Fishes swim in water clear,
Birds fly up into the air,
Serpents creep along the ground,
Boys and girls run round and round.

A New Home for Bear

Bear lived all alone on a dusty shelf in the playroom. His boy was grown up now and didn't have time for toys anymore. Then, one day, the boy took him down and dusted him off.

"I think it's time you found a new home," he smiled. "I'm going to put you on the toy table at the school jumble sale."

Bear was very excited. He couldn't wait to find a new child to love. He sat on the toy table and smiled his best smile. But when a little girl reached over to pick up a china doll, she knocked him over and he fell to the ground.

Soon the jumble sale was over and the toy table was put away. No one noticed poor Bear all alone in the grass.

It grew dark and Bear shivered. But he was a brave teddy bear and wasn't afraid of the dark.

In the morning, the sun came up and shone on the pretty flowers. Bear smiled happily – especially when a little girl came by.

"What a happy bear!" she laughed when she saw him. And she picked him up and took him home. She gave him a bath and a ribbon for his neck. At last, Bear had found a new home.

Nine Bored Wolves

Nine bored wolves stand around and wait,
One goes hunting, then there are eight.
Eight bored wolves decide to do some tricks,
Two play 'Chase my Tail', then there are six.
Six bored wolves – they wouldn't hurt a flea,
Three find a trail to sniff, then there are three.
Three bored wolves decide to have some fun,
So they all play Wolf Chase... and then there are none.

The Turtle's Race With the Bear

One day, a bear was walking near a frozen pond when he spotted a turtle's head sticking out of a hole in the ice.

"Good morning, slow creature," the bear called.

"Why are you calling me slow?" the turtle asked.

"Everyone knows you are the slowest of all the animals," the bear declared. "Anyone could beat you."

"Well let's find out," the turtle said. "Let's have a race."

The bear snorted with laughter at the thought that he could be beaten by a turtle, and he agreed to race the following morning. Soon after sunrise the turtle and the bear met at the pond. Animals had come from miles around to watch the race.

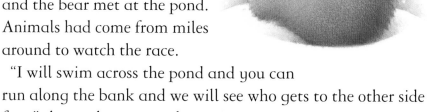

"I will swim across the pond and you can run along the bank and we will see who gets to the other side first," the turtle suggested.

"But how?" the bear asked. "The pond is covered in ice."

"I will make holes in the ice. Each time I reach a hole I will stick my head out," the turtle explained.

The bear and the turtle took up their positions, the bear on the bank and the turtle in the water, and when a hare gave the signal, the race began. Clouds of snow flew up from the bear's feet as he sped away. Meanwhile, the turtle ducked under the ice and, in no time at all, his head appeared at the next hole.

"Come on, bear!" he shouted, "I'm in front of you already!"

The bear ran even faster, but seconds later, the turtle's head popped up from the next hole. No matter how fast the bear ran, he couldn't keep up with the turtle.

By the time the bear finished the race, he could hardly walk, but the turtle was there waiting for him.

The bear was so exhausted and embarrassed at having been beaten that he staggered back home and didn't come out again until spring.

Once the bear and the other animals had left the pond, the turtle tapped on the ice and turtle heads popped up in all the holes in the ice. They belonged to the turtle's family, who all looked just like him.

"We've taught that bear a lesson," the turtle said. "He won't call us slow again!" And ever since then, the bear has slept through the winter until spring arrives.

Mythical Monster

The monster lay in the mud at the bottom of the lake. She was sad. Everything had changed. Once, she'd been the most famous monster in the world. But now only a few people bothered to stand around waiting for a glimpse of her.

The monster knew what had gone wrong: she'd been too mean with her appearances. Once every twenty years just wasn't enough. People had got bored waiting.

She knew what to do. She had to make a splash! She swam across the lake, her spotted back breaking the surface. But when she lifted her neck, she saw that the shore was empty. In the distance there was a campsite, but the people there weren't looking towards the lake. They were outside their tents, reading newspapers and cooking supper. No one was interested in her.

She'd have to show herself properly, she decided. She swam to the shore and lumbered into the middle of the campsite.

A woman walked out of a tent. "Hey kids, that's a great costume," she cried, when she saw the monster. "Wherever did you get it? Now have a wash. Supper'll be ready soon."

As the monster was walking sadly back to the lake, a boy

came along. He screamed. "It's the monster!" he shouted.

"I wouldn't bother yourself with all that," said the monster to the astonished boy. "No one believes in me any more."

"That's terrible," said the boy. "We'll have to think of something that will get people's attention. I know – why don't I row out onto the lake and then pretend to be in trouble. Then you can rescue me."

The boy rowed himself out onto the lake, then deliberately pushed the oars away. "Help! I'm going to drown!" he cried.

The campers came running to the shore. Right on cue, the monster reared up out of the water. A great wave engulfed the boat, tossing the boy into the water.

"The monster's attacking my son!" cried a woman.

"That isn't what I had in mind," thought the monster. She plucked the boy from the water with her huge jaws.

"It's eating my son!" cried the woman.

Holding the boy in her mouth, the monster swam to the shore and put him down in front of his mother.

"The monster's saved my son!" cried the woman. "It's a hero!"

Cameras were flashing everywhere. "That's enough for me," the monster thought. She dived to the bottom of the lake. "I'll lay low for a while," she said to herself. "Just for another twenty years or so. A monster can only take so much attention, after all."

Snap Holiday

One quiet, lazy morning, Claudia Crocodile was drifting down the river looking for fun. In the distance, she could see Mickey and Maxine Monkey playing on the riverbank.

"I'll give them a fright," decided Claudia. "It's always amusing to watch them run away!"

Sure enough, the *Snap! Snap!* of Claudia's strong jaws scared the little monkeys.

That afternoon, Claudia was feeling bored again, so she looked for someone else to frighten.

She saw Timmy Tiger on his own and crept up right behind him! *Snap! Snap!* went her great big jaws, right by Timmy's tail.

Timmy was trembling with terror. But Claudia didn't eat him, as he thought she would.

"Why haven't you eaten me?" asked Timmy timidly.

"I don't want to eat you. You're furry and yucky! I only snap to scare people. That's what crocodiles are meant to do."

"I never knew you could

be nice. I like you!
I think everyone would like you," said
Timmy, "if you could just be friendly,
instead of scary."

As Timmy and Claudia went along
together, they saw Mickey and Maxine,
trying to smash open some coconuts.

"Here's your chance," Timmy told
Claudia.

Claudia nodded and swam towards the
monkeys. *Snap! Snap!* As soon as they heard her, the
monkeys ran.

"It's all right," said Claudia, "I just want to help. Throw me
a coconut!"

The monkeys were uncertain but Mickey tossed his coconut
at Claudia's gaping jaws. *Snap! Snap! Snap!*

Quick as a flash, the coconut was open. "Gosh, Claudia,
thanks!" said an amazed Mickey.

Claudia opened Maxine's coconut, too.
Soon, everyone was happy sharing the
cool, refreshing milk and chomping on
chewy chunks of coconut.

But happiest of all was Claudia,
who had found that having friends
was so much more fun than scaring
them!

A Farmer Went Trotting

A farmer went trotting upon his grey mare,
Bumpety, bumpety, bump!
With his daughter behind so rosy and fair,
Lumpety, lumpety, lump!
A raven cried, "Croak!" They went tumbling down,
Bumpety, bumpety, bump!
The mare broke her knees and the farmer his crown,
Lumpety, lumpety, lump!
The mischievous raven flew laughing away,
Bumpety, bumpety, bump!
And vowed he would serve them the same the next day,
Lumpety, lumpety, lump!

Lark-bird

Lark-bird, lark-bird, soaring high,
Are you never weary
When you reach the empty sky?
Are the clouds not dreary?
Don't you sometimes long to be
A silent goldfish in the sea?
Goldfish, goldfish, diving deep,
Are you never sad, say
When you feel the cold waves creep?
Are you really glad, say?
Don't you sometimes long to sing
And be a lark-bird on the wing?

Dreamtime

What do creatures dream of
When they close their eyes?
Do they dream like you and I
Beneath the starry skies?
Do donkeys dream of pulling carts,
And munching bales of hay?

Do piglets dream of muck and mud,
And all the games they play?
Do buttercups and fresh green grass
Fill a cow's sweet dreams,
When they fall asleep at night
Beneath the moonlit beams?

And how do sheep fall asleep?
By counting dogs and cats?
Do kittens dream of bowls of cream,
And chasing mice and rats?

Do roosters dream of morning time,
And crowing very loud?
Or do they dream of bossing hens,
And strutting, oh, so proud?
What do creatures dream of
When they close their eyes?
Do they dream like you and I
Beneath the moonlit skies?

This Old Man

This old man, he played one;
He played knick-knack on a drum.

Chorus:
With a knick-knack, paddy whack,
Give a dog a bone;
This old man came rolling home.

This old man, he played two;
He played knick-knack on my shoe.

Chorus:
With a knick-knack, paddy whack,
Give a dog a bone;
This old man came rolling home.

This old man, he played three;
He played knick-knack on my knee.

Chorus:
With a knick-knack, paddy whack,
Give a dog a bone;
This old man came rolling home.

This old man, he played four;
He played knick-knack on my door.

Chorus:
With a knick-knack, paddy whack,
Give a dog a bone;
This old man came rolling home.

This old man, he played five;
He played knick-knack on my hive.

Sing the chorus!

Jack and the Beanstalk

Once upon a time there was a boy called Jack. He lived with his mother in a cottage. They were very poor.

One day, Jack's mother said, "We have no food left to eat and no money to buy it with. Take the cow to market and sell her."

So Jack took the cow to market. On the way, Jack met a very old man walking along the road.

"Where are you going?" asked the old man.

"I am going to market to sell the cow," said Jack.

The old man offered Jack five magic beans for the cow. Jack agreed and sold the cow, then took the beans home.

"I sold the cow for five magic beans," he told his mother.

"Five beans!" she said. She was cross! She threw the magic beans out of the window.

Then she sent Jack to bed without any supper.

In the morning, Jack woke up. He looked out of the window. There was a giant beanstalk. It went up, up into the sky.

Jack climbed up the beanstalk.

At the top, there was a giant castle. Jack knocked on the door. The door opened.

Jack went in. Everything in the castle was enormous. That was because a giant and his wife lived in the castle.

"Fee, fi, fo, fum!" said the giant. "I want my breakfast."
Jack was afraid.

"You must hide," said the giant's wife, "or my husband will
eat you."

Jack hid from the giant.

The giant sat down at the table. Then he
put a hen on the table.

"Hen, lay an egg!" said the giant. The
hen laid a golden egg.

"Here is your breakfast," said the
giant's wife.

His wife gave him a very big breakfast.

The giant ate his breakfast. Then he felt
very sleepy. "Time for my nap," he said.

Soon he was fast asleep.

"A golden egg!" said Jack. "I will take the hen.
She will lay golden eggs and make us rich."

"Cluck!" said the hen. The giant woke up! Jack
ran to the beanstalk. The giant ran after him.

But Jack got his axe and chopped down
the beanstalk.

When the beanstalk fell to the ground,
the giant came crashing down with it.
That was the end of him!

Then the hen laid a golden egg.

And soon Jack and his mother weren't poor
any more!

Apple Picking

One day, Gloria the pig was feeling hungry. She gazed at the juicy red apples on the tree on the other side of the wall. They looked delicious! The problem was, Gloria was just too small to reach them.

"Maybe I could grab one from up on the wall," she thought, scrambling up. CRASH! Gloria fell to the ground.

"Maybe I can knock one down with this stick," she oinked, waving it in the air. But she just ended up covered in leaves.

"Maybe you can peck one down, Magpie," suggested Gloria. Magpie tried his best, but that didn't work either. The apples kept falling on the wrong side of the wall.

"I give up," sighed Gloria. Just then, Farmer Sam arrived.

"You look fed up, Gloria," he said. "What can I do to cheer you up?"

Farmer Sam looked around and then had a brilliant idea. He went into the orchard, picked a bucketful of juicy red apples, and poured them into Gloria's trough.

Gloria squealed with delight. She was as happy as a pig in an orchard!

Sowing Corn

One for the mouse,
One for the crow,
One to rot,
One to grow.

A Horse and Cart

A horse and cart
Had Billy Smart,
To play with when it pleased him;
The cart he'd load
By the side of the road,
And be happy if no one teased him.

An Elephant

When people call this beast to mind
They marvel more and more
At such a little tail behind
So large a trunk before.

Naja Keeps Cool

It was a scorching hot day, and Naja the Cobra was so hot that she didn't know what to do with herself.

"I'll have to find ssssomewhere cool to sleep," she hissed. She looked around and saw a big rock. "I can find sssshade under that," she thought. But as soon as she touched the rock she spat out an angry hiss. It had been in the sun for so long that it was burning hot.

Naja slithered over to a pile of leaves. "I'll hide beneath these," she thought. But when she tried to crawl under she was chased out by an army of angry ants.

By now Naja was so hot and sleepy that she could barely move. Then she saw the house...

Slowly, she slithered through the open door – but quickly raced back out again with an angry woman on her tail.

"Get out," yelled the woman, thumping Naja with a broom. Naja slithered away, down the steps, and into the cellar.

"Ahh!" she sighed. "This is lovely." Then she spotted a cool water pitcher. Slithering over, she wrapped herself around the pitcher.

"Wonderful!" hissed Naja happily. At last she could sleep in peace.

What's in a Name?

One morning, Tailorbird was busy flittering around the forest when a curious little mongoose wandered along.

The mongoose watched the busy bird gathering things, and then coughed to get her attention. "Excuse me? Why are you called Tailorbird?" he asked. "If you ask me, you should be called Busy bird."

"Cheeup! Cheeup!" chirped Tailorbird. "Sorry, I'm too busy to talk right now. You'll just have to wait and see."

So the mongoose sat down to watch. First Tailorbird used her sharp beak to pierce tiny holes in two big leaves. Then she threaded a long piece of spider's silk through the holes to join the leaves together. Next she lined the cradle of leaves with soft wool to make it warm and cosy. When she was finished, she poked her head out of her cosy new nest.

"Do you still wonder why I'm called Tailorbird?" she chirped.

Mongoose smiled and shook his head. "No!" he laughed. "The answer is plain to see! It's because you are so good at sewing, just like a tailor who makes clothes!"

Muddypaws!

It was a special day for Ben. He had a new puppy!

"I'll teach you all the things I know," said Ben. "But first I need to choose a name for you. I'll need to think hard about it. It has to be just perfect."

"I don't really mind what name you choose, as long as you give me lots of cuddles," thought the puppy.

Ben looked around his bedroom to see if he could find an idea for the perfect puppy name.

"I'll look in my storybook," he said, but none of the names in the book were right.

"I think I'll let you hunt for names," thought the new puppy. "I'd rather look behind that flowerpot."

The little puppy crept over... He sniffed...

... and then he climbed. He didn't mean to knock the flowerpot over, but...

Oops! That's just what he did. He made muddy paw prints everywhere.

"Let's go to the park. I might be able to think of a good name there," said Ben.

"I'd rather look behind that tree," thought the little puppy. So he ran... and he ran.

He didn't mean to jump in the mud, but... **squelch!** That's just what he did. He made muddy paw prints everywhere.

Ben's neighbours were having a party in their back garden.

"One of the guests might be able to think of a good name for you," said Ben. "Let's go and ask them."

"I'd rather look in the pond," thought the new puppy. So he leaned over... and he leaned over a little bit more. He didn't mean to fall in the pond, but... **splosh!** That's just what he did.

He made muddy paw prints everywhere.

"We'd better go home and clean you up," said Ben.

"I'd rather go digging in the garden," thought the new puppy.

So he dug... and he dug... and he dug. This time he found lots of things... a lost ring... an old wrench ...and a toy car that Ben had lost. He didn't mean to bring all that mud indoors, but... pitter patter... that's just what he did, all over the kitchen floor. He made muddy paw prints everywhere.

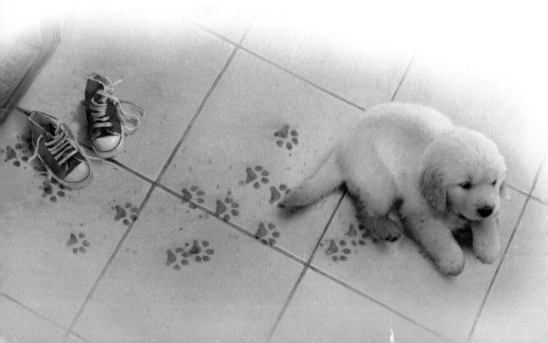

And he didn't mean to find a name for himself at last, but... guess what? That's *just* what he did!

"You are the muddiest, funniest puppy there ever was. There's only one name for you," laughed Ben.

Can you guess what it is?

"Muddypaws!"

The Lion and the Mouse

One day, a lion was fast asleep in his den when he was woken by something running across his face. The lion lazily opened one eye and was surprised to see a little mouse right in front of his nose. As fast as lightning, the lion's paw shot out and caught the mouse.

"How dare you run across the face of the king of beasts!" the lion roared. "You will pay for that with your life!"

The lion opened his enormous mouth and was just about to swallow the mouse, when he heard the creature squeaking.

"Please don't eat me, sir," the mouse pleaded. "If you forgive me and let me go, I will do something for you one day, to repay your kindness."

The lion laughed and laughed at the thought that a creature as small and unimportant as a mouse could ever do anything to help the king of beasts.

"You repay me?" the lion spluttered. "I can't imagine that."

But, because the lion had just eaten a big meal and he found the mouse's plea so funny, he let the little creature go.

Some time later, the lion was stalking a zebra when he became caught in a net that had been laid on the ground by hunters. The lion tried to free himself, but the more he struggled, the more he got tangled in the ropes. Soon, he was too exhausted to struggle anymore, or even roar for help.

The lion had almost given up hope of ever escaping, when who should come by but the little mouse he had let go earlier.

"Let me help you," squeaked the little mouse, climbing onto the lion's shoulder. And he began to nibble through the ropes with his sharp teeth. Soon he had bitten through most of the knots, and the lion wriggled free.

Before running off, the lion thanked the little mouse.

"I am very grateful to you, my friend," he said. "You have taught me an important lesson: no act of kindness is wasted, however small it may be."

Aesop's moral: Little friends can turn out to be great friends.

The Bumble Bee!

The bumble bee is small and round,
It flies about above the ground,
With stripes of yellow on its back,
Or maybe it has stripes of black!
Two little wings to help it zoom,
So it can go from bloom to bloom,
Collecting pollen on its feet,
To make some honey, sweet to eat.
But whatever else it does,
The noise it makes is...
Buzz! Buzz! Buzz!

Guinea-pig

Once there was a guinea-pig,
He was not small, he was not big.
He always walked upon his feet,
His favourite food was greens to eat.
Sometimes he tried to run away,
Sometimes he would stay to play.
And when he ran, he ran so fast,
You barely saw him running past.
He sometimes called quite noisily,
And often squeaked "Hello!" to me.

Tiny Bear

Tiny Bear was a very curious bear, who was always asking lots of questions: "Why is the sky blue? Where does the night go? How do worms wiggle?"

"Goodness!" Daddy would laugh. "So many questions!" But, of course, he and Mummy Bear always did their best to give Tiny Bear an answer. Knowing the right answer wasn't always easy, though.

One day, the Bear family was strolling through the forest when Tiny Bear had a funny thought.

"What does the world look like upside down?" he asked.

Mummy and Daddy Bear looked at each other and smiled.

"I can't really tell you!" laughed Mummy Bear. "You are going to have to answer that question for yourself!"

"But how?" asked Tiny Bear.

"I'll show you as soon as we get home," replied Mummy Bear.

Tiny Bear ran home as fast as he could. "Hurry up," he cried. "I want to know what the world looks like upside down."

"Right," panted Mummy Bear. "Stand up straight and

stretch your arms up above your head."

"What's that got to do with what the world looks like upside down?" laughed Tiny Bear.

"You'll see in a minute," smiled Mummy Bear. "Point your right foot in front of you, and fall forwards until your hands touch the ground. Then kick your legs into the air and try to hold your legs up straight."

"But I'll fall," squealed Tiny Bear.

"Don't worry," said Mummy Bear. "I'll hold your legs."

Tiny Bear did as Mummy Bear instructed, and could soon do a handstand all by himself.

"What does the world looks like now?" asked Mummy Bear.

"All topsy turvy," laughed Tiny Bear. "This is fun! Why don't you do a handstand and see for yourself?"

"All right," laughed Mummy Bear. "But Daddy Bear will have to do one, too."

The Fox and the Stork

Once upon a time a fox decided to play a trick on his neighbour, the stork.

"Would you like to come and have supper with me?" he asked her one morning.

The stork was surprised by the invitation, because the fox had never been friendly to her before, but she happily accepted. He looked like a well-fed beast, and she was sure he would provide her with a good meal.

Every now and then, through the day, the stork caught the mouth-watering smell of the soup that the fox was preparing. By the time she arrived at his home she was feeling very hungry – which was exactly what the fox wanted.

"Enjoy your meal," said the crafty fox, ladling the soup into a shallow bowl. Of course, the fox was able to lap his up easily, but the stork could only dip the tip of her bill

into the soup. She wasn't able to drink a single drop!

"Mmm, that was delicious," said the fox when he had slurped up the soup. "I see you don't have much of an appetite, so I will have yours, too."

The poor stork went home feeling hungrier than ever and was determined to take her revenge on the sly fox for playing such a mean trick. So the following week, she went to see him.

"Thank you for inviting me to supper last week," she said. "Now I would like to return the favour. Please come and dine with me this evening."

The fox was a little suspicious that the stork might want to get her own back, but he didn't see how she could possibly play a trick on him. After all, he was known for his cunning, and very few creatures had ever managed to outwit him.

All day long the fox looked forward to his supper, and by the evening he was very hungry. As he approached the stork's home he caught the appetising aroma of a fish stew and started to lick his lips.

But when the stork served the stew it was in a tall pot with a very narrow neck. The stork could reach the food easily with her long bill, but the fox could only lick the rim of the pot and sniff the tempting smell. Much as he didn't want to, the fox had to admit he had been outsmarted – and went home with an empty stomach!

Aesop's moral: One bad turn deserves another.

The Elves and the Shoemaker

Once, there was a shoemaker and his wife who were very poor. The day came when the shoemaker had only one piece of leather left, so he cut out one last pair of shoes and went to bed with a heavy heart.

That night, two **helpful** elves came out to play. They saw the leather, and sewed it very neatly into a pair of shoes.

The next morning, the shoemaker came downstairs and was **amazed** to find the finished shoes. "What delicate work!" he said.

Just then, a woman came into the shoe shop. When she saw the shoes with their beautiful stitching, she tried them on and they fitted perfectly. "These shoes are just right," she said, and gave the shoemaker twice the money he usually got. The shoemaker had enough money to buy a big piece of leather.

That evening, the shoemaker cut out some boots.

During the night, the two elves came out to work again. They saw the leather and sewed a beautiful pair of boots.

The next morning, the shoemaker was happy to find the boots. "What wonderful work!" he said.

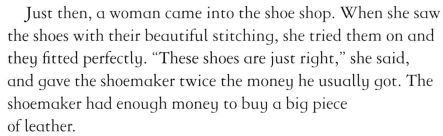

Just then, a man came into the shoe shop. He took off his shoes and tried on the boots. "These boots are just right," he said. He paid handsomely for them, so the shoemaker bought a **bigger** piece of leather, which he used to cut out a pair of shoes and a pair of boots.

"Who is making the shoes and boots?" asked the shoemaker's wife. "Let's see if we can find out!"

When it was time for bed, the shoemaker and his wife hid. Soon, the elves came out and sewed the shoes and the boots.

"What **kind** elves," the shoemaker said to his wife. "How can we thank them?"

"Let's make them some shoes!" said the shoemaker's wife.

So the shoemaker got his **finest** piece of leather and they made two pairs of tiny shoes.

That night, the shoemaker and his wife hid, and watched as the elves tried on the tiny shoes – they fitted **perfectly!**

The two elves danced happily away into the night.

After the elves had gone, lots of people came to buy shoes and boots.

The shoemaker and his wife were never poor again.

Winter Nights

Blow, wind, blow! Drift the flying snow!
Send it twirling, whirling overhead!
There's a bedroom in a tree,
Where, snug as snug can be,
The squirrel nests in his cosy bed.
Shriek, wind, shriek!
Make the branches creak!
Battle with the boughs till break of day!
In a snow cave warm and tight,
Through the icy winter night,
The rabbit sleeps the peaceful hours away.
Call, wind, call! In doorway and in hall!
Straight from the mountain white and wild!
Soft purrs the cat, on her fluffy mat,
And beside her nestles close her furry child.
Scold, wind, scold, so bitter and so bold!
Shake the windows with your tap, tap, tap!
With half-shut, dreamy eyes,
The drowsy baby lies,
Cuddled close in his mother's lap.

Gee up, Horsey

Gee up, horsey,
Off we go,
Clippety cloppety,
Nice and slow.
Clippety cloppety,
Down the lane,
All the way,
Then back again.

A Horse and a Flea

A horse and a flea and three blind mice,
Were sitting on a corner playing dice.
The horse he slipped and fell on the flea,
"Whoops!" said the flea, "there's a horsie on me!"

A Black-nosed Kitten

A black-nosed kitten will slumber all day,
A white-nosed kitten is ever-glad to play,
A yellow-nosed kitten will answer to your call,
And a grey-nosed kitten I wouldn't have at all!

Pretty Cow

Pretty cow, give me some milk,
And I will give you a gown of silk;
A gown of silk and a silver tee,
If you will give your milk for me.

Bow, Wow, Wow!

Bow, wow, wow! Whose dog art thou?
Little Tom Tinker's dog,
Bow, wow, wow.

The Elephant

The elephant has a trunk for a nose,
And up and down is the way it goes.
He wears such a saggy, baggy hide!
Do you think two elephants would fit inside?

The Rooster

The rooster's on the roof blowing his horn;
The bull's in the barn threshing the corn;
The maids in the meadows are making hay;
The ducks in the river are swimming away.

How Butterflies Came to Be

One day, a long time ago, Elder Brother, the spirit of goodness, was out walking. The summer was over, the sky was blue, and everywhere he looked he saw the colours of autumn.

Soon Elder Brother arrived at a village where the women were grinding corn and children were playing happily together. He sat down feeling very content, as he enjoyed the beautiful autumn colours and the sound of birdsong.

Suddenly, Elder Brother became sad. "It will be winter soon," he thought. "The colourful autumn leaves will shrivel and fall, and the flowers will fade."

Elder Brother tried to think of a way to keep the autumn colours, so that everyone could enjoy them for longer.

Wherever he went, Elder Brother always carried a bag. Now he opened it up and started to fill it with the colours he saw all around him.

He took gold from a ray of sunlight and blue from the sky. He collected shiny black from a woman's hair and white from the cornmeal. He took green from the pine needles, red and yellow from the leaves, and purple and orange from the flowers.

When all the colours were in the bag, Elder Brother shook it. Then he thought of something else. He heard the birds singing and added their songs to the bag.

Elder Brother called the children over.

"I have a surprise for you!" he told them.
"Take this bag and open it."

The children opened the bag, and hundreds of colourful butterflies flew out. How the children laughed with joy! The women came over to see the butterflies too, and so did the men who had been working in the fields. Everyone stretched out their hands so the butterflies could land on them, and the butterflies started to sing as they fluttered around.

The people were delighted, but the birds were angry. One bird perched on Elder Brother's shoulder.

"Why have you given our songs to the butterflies?" the bird asked. "We were each given our own song and now you've given them away to creatures that have more beautiful colours than we do."

Elder Brother agreed and apologised to the birds. He took the songs away from the butterflies and gave them back to the birds. And that is how butterflies came to be – and why they are silent.

Hippo Stays Awake

It was a very hot day in the jungle.

"It's too warm to do anything except snooze," thought Hatty Hippo, and she lay down by the waterhole.

Suddenly, the ground began to shake. *Thud, thud, thud!*

"It's only me!" trumpeted Effie Elephant. "I've just come for a quick shower to cool myself down."

Effie stood in the waterhole and sprayed water all over her back. *Slop! Slosh!*

The air was suddenly filled with loud cries.

"*Wheeee!*" It was a troupe of monkeys swinging through the trees. "Anyone for a water fight?" they called loudly.

"*Squawk, squawk!* Yes please!" the parrots shrieked. *Splosh! Splash! Whee! Squawk!*

Hatty groaned. How would she ever get to sleep now?

"*Quiet!*" yelled Hatty, louder than any of the other animals. All the noise stopped at once.

"Sorry, Hatty," whispered Effie. "You only had to say something." One by one, the animals tiptoed away.

Finally, the jungle was silent. "Aaaahh!" yawned Hatty, settling down. "Now I'm on my own, I'll get a little bit of peace at last!"

The Big Blue Egg

One morning, Little Brown Hen found a strange thing in the farmyard. It was big, blue and round. Little Brown Hen walked slowly round the big blue thing. She sniffed it, tapped it with her beak, and listened.

"Well, it's round like an egg," she said. "So it must be an egg. I'll keep it warm until it hatches."

Little Brown Hen settled down to wait for the egg to hatch. She waited… and waited… and waited… but nothing happened.

"Perhaps it isn't warm enough," she worried, giving the egg a nudge with her beak. Oops! The big blue egg toppled out of the nest and began to bounce away.

Boing! Boing! Boing! The egg bounced across the farmyard. "Stop that egg!" cried Little Brown Hen, running after it as fast as she could.

Up jumped Sheeba the sheepdog. She caught the runaway egg between her paws.

"I've been looking for this all day," barked Sheeba. "Thank you for finding it for me!"

"I didn't know that dogs laid eggs!" said Little Brown Hen.

"It's not an egg, silly," laughed Sheeba. "It's my puppy's favourite bouncy ball!"

Lonely Whale

"I wish I had someone to play with," said Whale. He was splashing around by himself in the sea.

"Hello, Whale! Want to play?" asked Seahorse, jumping out from under the rocks. But Seahorse was so small, Whale didn't hear him.

Two dolphins began leaping to and fro across Whale's back. "Play with us, Whale!" they cried. But Whale was so big, he didn't notice them.

Then three fish floated by. "Play with us, Whale!" they said. But the fish were so far away, Whale didn't see them.

Whale found Eel wriggling around the rocks. "I'd like to wriggle like that," said Whale. "But I'm so big and clumsy, I can't do anything," said Whale, sadly.

"But you're the biggest animal in the sea. Everyone loves you," said Eel. "Have a look behind you!"

Whale turned around and saw all the fish in the sea!

"Please play, Whale," they cried.

"I'm the luckiest whale in the whole world!" said Whale, and he swam off to join his friends.

Sssssh!

It was the middle of the night. All of a sudden, Kitten's tummy began to rumble.

"I'm really hungry!" said Kitten. "I've just got to go to the kitchen and find something to eat."

Kitten tried to quietly jump to the floor, but he landed on Puppy's tail instead.

"*Ow!*" cried Puppy.

"*Sssssh!*" whispered Kitten. "You'll wake everyone up!"

Kitten tiptoed down the hall…

"*Boo!*" shouted Rabbit, hopping up.

"*Sssssh!*" whispered Kitten. "You'll wake everyone up!"

Kitten crept through the living room and was startled by a noise under the sofa.

"Who's there?" asked Kitten, nervously.

"*Squeak! Squeak!*" squeaked Hamster.

"*Sssshh!*" whispered Kitten. "You'll wake everyone up!"

"*Meeeow!*" howled Kitten when he reached the kitchen at last. There was a fat little mouse eating out of his bowl!

"*Crash!*" went the bowl, and the dishes, and the saucepans, as Kitten chased the mouse all over the kitchen.

And after all that loud noise, who do you think woke up? Everyone!

The Queen's Pudding

Jim was the youngest, smallest and most hard-worked kitchen boy in the kitchens of the Queen of Hungerbert.

People shouted at him all day long: "Take this to the Queen!" "The Princess needs this now!" "Quickly!" "Move!"

One day the cook shouted at Jim, as usual.

"Take this pudding to the Queen! Now!" she said, giving Jim a dish of bananas and custard.

Jim took it to the Queen. The Queen took a bite.

"I like banana," she said. "But I don't like custard."

Jim went back to the kitchen.

Cook made jelly and ice cream. Jim took it to the Queen.

The Queen took a bite. "I like ice cream," she said. "But I don't like the jelly."

Cook made apple pie and cream.

"I like cream," said the Queen. "But I don't like pie."

"Oh dear!" said Cook. "The Queen only likes banana, ice cream and cream."

"That makes a banana split!" said Jim.

"You might just be right, Jim," said Cook. She made a banana split.

Jim took it to the Queen. She took a bite.

"I love it!" she said.

Jim went back to the kitchen and told Cook.

"Well done, Jim!" said Cook.

Row, Row, Row Your Boat

Row, row, row your boat,
Gently down the stream,
Merrily, merrily, merrily, merrily,
Life is but a dream.

Jay-bird

Jay-bird, jay-bird, sittin' on a rail,
Pickin' his teeth with the end of his tail;
Mulberry leaves and calico sleeves –
All school teachers are hard to please.

Spin, Dame

Spin, dame, spin,
Your bread you must win;
Twist the thread and break it not,
Spin, dame, spin.

The Robin and the Wren

The robin and the wren,
They fought upon the porridge pan;
But before the robin got a spoon,
The wren had eaten the porridge down.

The Mouse's Lullaby

Oh, rock-a-bye, baby mouse, rock-a-bye, so!
When baby's asleep to the baker's I'll go,
And while he's not looking I'll pop from a hole,
And bring to my baby a fresh penny roll.

Bow-wow

Bow-wow, says the dog,
Mew, mew, says the cat,
Grunt, grunt, goes the hog,
And squeak goes the rat.
Tu-whu, says the owl,
Caw, caw, says the crow,
Quack, quack, says the duck,
And what cuckoos say you know.

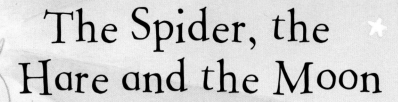

The Spider, the Hare and the Moon

The moon felt very sad. She knew that people on Earth were afraid of the dark, and she wanted to let them know that it was nothing to be scared of. She had no way of speaking to them herself, so she called on her friend the spider.

"Please take a message to everyone on Earth," she said to him. "Tell them that the world will always be in darkness at night, but there is no need to be afraid. I will be here to light their way."

The spider started to climb down the moonbeams to get back down to Earth. On the way, he bumped into the hare.

"Where are you going?" the hare asked.

"The moon has asked me to give an important message to all the people on Earth," the spider explained.

"Oh, you're so slow, it will take you much too long to get there," the hare said. "Let me take the message. I'm much faster than you. I'm sure if the moon said it was important she would want the people to hear it as quickly as possible. Tell me what the message is and I will give it to everyone on Earth."

"Well, I suppose the moon would want the people to hear her message as quickly as possible," the spider agreed. "Tell them the moon said that the world will always be in darkness …"

"Right," said the hare. "Tell the people on Earth that the world will always be in darkness."

And before the spider could finish, the hare had bounded off.

"Wait, wait," the spider shouted after him. "I haven't finished." But the hare had already disappeared.

The spider decided to go back and tell the moon what had happened. Otherwise she would wonder why the people on Earth were still scared.

Meanwhile, on Earth, the hare was busy telling all the people that the world would always be in darkness. And once he had delivered the message, he proudly went back to let the moon know what he had done.

Of course, the moon was furious with the hare – so furious in fact, that she sent him away and wouldn't speak to him ever again.

And the spider? The busy little spider is still trying to carry the moon's message to all the people on Earth as he spins his webs in the corners of our rooms.

The Magic Sky

One icy Arctic night, Lila and Poko the polar bear cubs were getting ready for bed. It was freezing outside, but it was cosy and warm inside their den. The two cubs snuggled down beside their mother and closed their eyes. They were almost asleep, when they heard a noise outside.

"Psst! Lila! Poko!" said a voice. It was their friend Tiki the Arctic hare.

"Come outside! Quickly!" whispered Tiki. "There is something I want to show you. Something very peculiar is happening. I think there must be magic in the air."

"What's going on?" yawned Mother Bear sleepily.

"Something magical is happening," replied Tiki. "I can't describe it. You must come and see for yourself."

"Ah," smiled Mother Bear. "I think I know what it is. Let's all go and take a look together."

The three sleepy polar bears crawled out of their den and padded across the icy snow. Lila and Poko looked around in surprise.

Everything looked so different. The icy landscape was bathed in a strange glow.

"Look up," whispered Tiki.

The polar bear cubs looked up and gasped in amazement. Something very strange was happening in the sky above. It was full of dancing lights, swirling and twirling around above their heads. They all stared in wonder, unable to speak at first.

"It's beautiful!" gasped Poko eventually.

"What's happening?" asked Lila.

"It's the Northern Lights!" said Mother Bear.

"Is it magic?" asked Poko excitedly. "We love magic."

Mother Bear thought for a while and then smiled.

"Yes," she agreed. "It's the magic of nature!"

Winnie's Big Egg

It was springtime, and the sun shone brightly over River Farm. Winnie the duck sat on the riverbank and quacked impatiently. She had been sitting on her nest for weeks, but not one of her six eggs had hatched. Winnie shifted around and ruffled her feathers. She turned over her eggs and polished each one. She adored her eggs, but she was beginning to wonder if they would ever hatch. Then, suddenly, there was a CRACK!

Out popped a tiny, fluffy duckling. Winnie was delighted.

Soon the other eggs began to crack, and Winnie was surrounded by five fluffy ducklings. Only the biggest egg remained.

Winnie rolled the big egg beneath her plump chest and

warmed it with her soft feathers. She waited and waited, but the egg didn't hatch.

"Why don't you leave it?" suggested the cow. "You've got five fine little ducklings. That one is obviously no good."

"No," quacked Winnie, wrapping her wings around the egg.

"I don't think that egg even belongs to you," clucked the wise old chicken, who knew a thing or two about eggs. "It's much too big to be a duck egg."

"Yes," neighed the horse. "I've heard about birds leaving their eggs in other birds' nests. It's a terrible thing."

But Winnie just sat on the last egg and waited.

Then, one sunny afternoon, there was a loud CRACK! Winnie quacked with excitement. All the farm animals gathered around to see the new arrival.

"I bet it's a baby goose," whispered the chicken.

"I think it will be a baby swan," neighed the horse.

Everyone held their breath as out popped ... two tiny ducklings. It was twins! Winnie quacked with pride. She had always known the big egg was special. Now she had seven perfect little ducklings.

"Come on, boys and girls," she called as she proudly led her babies down to the river.

The Penguin Who Wanted to Sparkle

One moonlit night, Mummy penguin's egg went CRACK! A tiny beak appeared, a head, then two wings and two orange feet. A fluffy little penguin chick called Pip hopped out.

"Pretty sparkles!" she squeaked, as she gazed up at the sparkly stars in the sky. Then Pip saw a funny fish leap out of the ocean waves – SPLASH! It was all shiny and sparkly. "I want to sparkle, too," she squeaked.

Soon it began to snow. Pip watched the sparkling snowflakes floating down. "If I catch some, I can sprinkle them on my feathers," she thought. "Then I will sparkle, too."

Pip ran around, trying to catch the snowflakes, but they just melted on her wings. Then she found a bank of powdery white snow, twinkling in the moonlight. "Now I will sparkle!" she cried, rolling over in the snowy drift.

But the moon disappeared behind a cloud, and Pip's feathers didn't sparkle one tiny bit.

"Maybe I can catch a sparkly star,"

thought Pip, jumping up and down. But she couldn't reach one, no matter how hard she tried.

"What are you doing, Pip?" asked the other penguins.

"I'm trying to catch some sparkles," Pip explained.

Just then a friendly whale swam by. "All that jumping and rolling around looks very tiring!" he laughed. "Why don't you come and slide on my back instead?"

Everyone agreed that this was a wonderful idea – even Pip. One by one, the penguins whooshed down the whale's back and landed in the glittering sea. SPLASH! Pip hopped out and shook her wet feathers in the sunshine.

"Look!" cried the other penguins. "You're sparkling all over!"

"So that's how you sparkle," cried Pip, dancing in the snow. "By having fun in the sun. Come on, everyone. Let's do it again!"

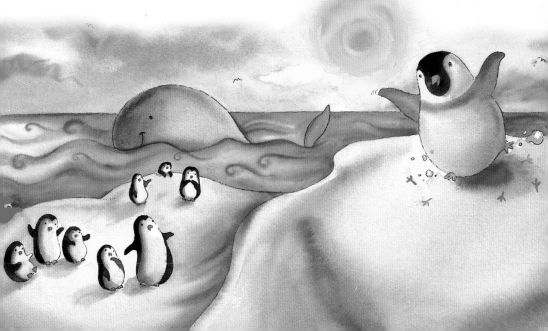

It's Raining, It's Pouring

It's raining, it's pouring,
The old man is snoring;
He went to bed and bumped his head
And couldn't get up in the morning.

Blow, Wind, Blow

Blow, wind, blow! And go, mill, go!
That the miller may grind his corn;
That the baker may take it,
And into rolls make it,
And send us some hot in the morn.

Rain, Rain, Go Away

Rain, rain,
Go away,
Come again
Another day.

Sneeze on Monday

Sneeze on Monday, sneeze for danger;
Sneeze on Tuesday, kiss a stranger;
Sneeze on Wednesday, get a letter;
Sneeze on Thursday, something better;
Sneeze on Friday, sneeze for sorrow;
Sneeze on Saturday, see your sweetheart tomorrow.

Jackanory

I'll tell you a story
Of Jackanory,
And now my story's begun;
I'll tell you another
Of Jack his brother,
And now my story's done.

Little Wind

Little wind, blow on the hill-top;
Little wind, blow down the plain;
Little wind, blow up the sunshine;
Little wind, blow off the rain.

The Fox's Tail

One day, a fox was out walking when he heard a loud snap and felt a sudden pain in his tail. The poor fox had been caught in a hunter's trap. He looked behind him and saw that his tail was completely stuck. No matter how much he struggled, he just couldn't free it.

"Help!" he shouted. "Ouch!" he cried. "Owwww!" he howled. But no one came to help him.

At last, the fox pulled and pulled with all his strength and managed to break free, but when he looked back, he saw that his tail had been left behind in the jaws of the trap.

"What will all the other foxes think when they see me?" thought the fox. "They'll all laugh at me. I don't even look like a fox without my tail. It's so embarrassing!"

For days the fox hid away in his den and only came out at night when no one could see him. Then he came up with an idea. He called a meeting of all the foxes in the area.

The foxes gathered in a clearing. Sure enough, as soon as they saw the fox without his tail, they started to laugh.

"I've called you together to tell you about my wonderful discovery," the fox announced, struggling to be heard above their laughter. "Over the years, I've felt that my tail was nothing but a nuisance. It was always getting muddy, and when it rained it got all wet and took ages to dry. It slowed me down when I was hunting, and I never knew what to do with it when I was lying down. So I decided it was time to get rid of it, and I can't tell you how much easier it is to move around without all that extra weight dragging along behind me. I cut my tail off, and I recommend that you all follow my example and do the same."

One of the older foxes stood up. "If I had lost my tail like you, I might have agreed with what you are saying," he said. "But until such a thing happens, I will be very happy to keep my tail, and I am sure everyone else here feels the same."

The other foxes all stood up and proudly waved their tails in the air as they walked away.

Aesop's moral: Do not listen to the advice of someone who is trying to bring you down to their level.

131

Doctor Finley Pig

Finley was a very happy pig.
Life just couldn't be better.
"It's alright for you!"
said Agatha Chicken,
who was always sticking
her beak in other people's
business. "This is a busy farm,
lazybones," she clucked.

"But I'm not a lazybones," replied the happy little porker.
"I'm Finley."

"Don't be cheeky!" Agatha flapped her wings and squawked
until Finley ran away.

Finley sat under a tree to think. Taking mud baths was
a lovely way to spend your time, but he did want to be a big
help on the busy farm, too. What would he be good at?

Mummy Pig was puzzled. "Where are you going with all
those things, Finley?" she asked.

"I'm not Finley, I'm Doctor Pig!"
replied Finley. "And I'm
late for my first patient.
What seems to be the
trouble, Mrs Moo?"

Mrs Moo mooed.
"Don't say moo, say
ahhh!" said Finley.

"Finley, there's nothing wrong with my leg," said Mrs Moo, as Finley tried to tie a bandage around it.

"Hold still for Doctor Pig, please!" said Finley.

Chester Sheep was not good at having his heart listened to – he wouldn't stop munching.

The geese, Heidi and Dora, refused their medicine.

And Tilly the sheepdog? Well, she just ran away...

Being a doctor was really hard work, but the most difficult patients of all were the chickens. There were just so many of them, and they all wanted to be first in the queue.

At the end of a long day, Mummy Pig was pleased to see Finley.

"I'm very good at being a doctor," said Finley. "But I'm even better at being me."

Life just couldn't be better!

Little Lamb Gets Lost

One day, Little Lamb was grazing in the meadow when Huey, his oldest brother, began to bleat.

"Have you seen how green the grass is on other side of the hedge?" he called. "It looks much juicier than the grass here."

"Baa," agreed Duey, Little Lamb's other brother. "I'm hungry. Let's go over there and eat. Come on, Little Lamb."

Little Lamb wasn't sure he wanted to leave his lovely meadow home.

"But the grass here is delicious," he said. **"It's the best grass in the world!"**

Huey and Duey wouldn't listen. They pushed their way through a hole in the hedge and trotted off. Little Lamb had no choice but to follow.

Huey and Duey trotted on and on, stopping every now and then to munch the grass. They didn't bother to look where they were going. They just sniffed the air and trotted to where the grass smelled sweetest.

Twice they had to paddle across a stream, and once they even pushed through a thick hedge. They didn't let anything get in their way.

At last, as darkness began to fall, they found a place with the juiciest grass of all. They stopped and looked around.

"Where are we?" they baaed. But it was so dark that they couldn't see a thing.

"Ooooh," cried Huey. "We're lost."

"How will we ever find our way back home?" wailed Duey. "We'll have to stay here for the night."

Little Lamb began to cry. "I want to go home," he bleated.

Just then, a cloud shifted in the night sky and the silvery light of the moon shone down on the three sheep. Little Lamb looked around and saw that they were standing beside a big tree.

"I recognise that tree," he said.

"And I recognise that bush over there," added Huey.

"We're back in our meadow," said Duey. "Our noses led us all the way back home."

"Little Lamb was right, after all," laughed Huey. "Our meadow... has the best grass in the world!"

"Baaaaa," bleated Little Lamb in agreement. "Shall we have a little bedtime snack?"

Frog Goes Exploring

Frog had lived happily on the riverbank for so long that he was friends with everyone – from the smallest minnow to the finest swan. He couldn't wish for a better place to live. But Frog had a secret dream. He dreamed of finding out where the river went. He imagined that it led somewhere exciting – perhaps a great city or an exotic jungle, or maybe a sunny beach. So one winter, Frog got to work building himself a boat. He sawed and hammered all winter long, and by the spring his boat was ready.

After waving goodbye to all his friends, Frog set off on his great adventure. He hadn't been rowing for long when a head popped out of the river.

"Where are you going?" asked the fish.

"I'm going on a great journey to find the end of the river," Frog explained. And that is exactly what he told everyone he met as he glided slowly along.

All day, Frog rowed down the river, having a wonderful time. The sun shone down, and birds and animals called hello to him. He passed open fields, small villages and great towns. There was so much to see that Frog barely noticed the miles going by, and he never thought about stopping for a rest. On and on he rowed until, suddenly, he stopped with a THUD! The boat had hit dry land, and his journey was over!

Frog looked around with excitement. What fabulous place had he found? But he wasn't greeted by the sight of a grand city or a towering jungle, or even a busy beach. He hadn't arrived at a fabulous place. He had arrived at a small pond.

It wasn't at all what Frog had expected. But he wasn't disappointed. He waved to a friendly bluebird, and called hello to a curious bee. Then he sat back and smiled.

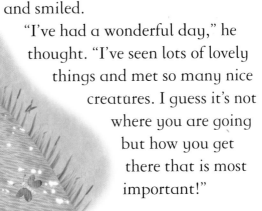

"I've had a wonderful day," he thought. "I've seen lots of lovely things and met so many nice creatures. I guess it's not where you are going but how you get there that is most important!"

The Animal Fair

I went to the animal fair,
All the birds and the beasts were there,
The big baboon by the light of the moon
Was combing his auburn hair.
The monkey bumped the skunk,
And sat on the elephant's trunk;
The elephant sneezed and fell to his knees,
And that was the end of the monkey,
monkey, monkey...

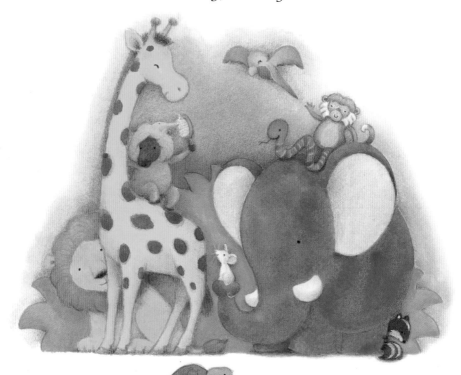

Creature Features

Here is the ostrich straight and tall,
Nodding his head above us all.
Here is the field mouse tiny and small,
Rolling himself into a ball.
Here is the spider scuttling around,
Treading so lightly on the ground.
Here are the birds that fly so high,
Spreading their wings across the sky.
Here are the children fast asleep,
And in the night the owls do peep,
"Toowhit toowhoo, toowhit toowhoo!"

Daisy's Big Adventure

Once upon a time there was a marmalade kitten called Daisy who belonged to a little boy named Charlie. Daisy was a very happy little kitten. When she wasn't having fun in the garden, she spent her days playing in Charlie's bedroom. She loved playing with Charlie's toys and knew every one of them by name. And after a hard day's playing, Daisy would curl up and go to sleep on Charlie's bed.

One morning Daisy awoke to find something new sitting on Charlie's bedroom floor. It was a big, square, wooden thing. "What can it be?" wondered Daisy. She sniffed the "thing" gingerly and prodded it with her paw. "Maybe it's a new place for me to sleep," she thought. And she leaped inside to try it out. But she leaped out again immediately. The "thing" was full of tiny people. They were dressed in fine clothes and looked very important. One of them was even riding a horse!

"Who are they and where have they come from?" she wondered. She hid behind the jack-in-the-box and watched to see what they would do. Daisy waited and waited, but the tiny people did not move. Even the horse stayed perfectly still.

"How strange," thought Daisy. She crept out from her hiding place and gave one of the people a nudge. The poor fellow fell to the ground and didn't move.

"I am sorry," she meowed. "I hope I haven't hurt you."

Just then, Charlie woke up. When he heard Daisy meowing he jumped out of bed and picked her up.

"What are you doing?" he laughed, giving her a hug. "Are you playing with my new castle and toy soldiers?'

"Ahhh," thought Daisy. "So that's why they don't move. They're toys!"

From that day on, the castle became Daisy's favourite toy. She liked nothing better than playing soldiers and kittens. But the game she enjoyed best was knights and dragons – with Daisy as the dragon, of course.

Ice Cool Duel

Angelino's Famous Ice Cream
Has a rival in town,
A juggling ice cream man called Bob,
Who'll bring his business down.

Bob, who's not such a nice fellow,
Says, "Angelino, I want you out,
We'll have a juggling contest,
And the winner keeps the route."

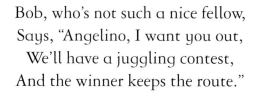

Angelino keeps his cool, though,
Knows that he will be just fine.
What goes up a plain old cone,
Comes down a lemon and lime.

Bob hates the thought of losing,
Reaches down towards his knees,
Juggles sixteen triple-dippers,
Tells Angelino, "Time to freeze!"

But Angelino's wise to Bob,
So he plays his final trick,
Bob falls, knocked out cold,
By a large vanilla brick!

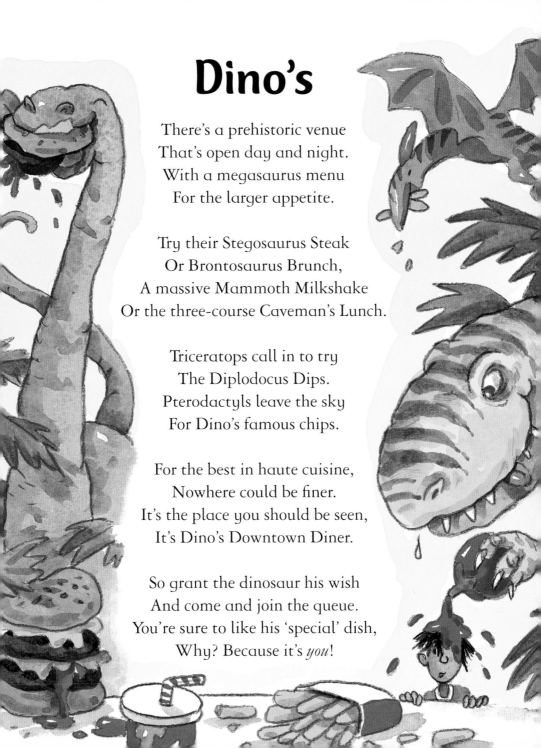

Dino's

There's a prehistoric venue
That's open day and night.
With a megasaurus menu
For the larger appetite.

Try their Stegosaurus Steak
Or Brontosaurus Brunch,
A massive Mammoth Milkshake
Or the three-course Caveman's Lunch.

Triceratops call in to try
The Diplodocus Dips.
Pterodactyls leave the sky
For Dino's famous chips.

For the best in haute cuisine,
Nowhere could be finer.
It's the place you should be seen,
It's Dino's Downtown Diner.

So grant the dinosaur his wish
And come and join the queue.
You're sure to like his 'special' dish,
Why? Because it's *you*!

The Vain Swan

Once upon a time four beautiful swans lived on a big river.
The swans were the best of friends and were very happy.
They looked so graceful and lovely that people always stopped
to admire them. Then one day, something happened. Felix, the
youngest swan, noticed his reflection for the first time. He was
very pleased with what he saw and began to boast about how
handsome
he was.

"Look at my
fine feathers,"
he said vainly.
"I have
the whitest
feathers of
any swan

on the river. I'm sure all the people come here to look at me.
They're not interested in ordinary swans, like the rest of you."

At first the older swans tried to ignore him. But Felix kept
staring at his reflection and remarking upon his beauty.
Before too long, the other swans got fed up and decided to
teach him a lesson.

"If people only come to see YOU," they honked, "then we
don't need to stay here. We can find somewhere else fit for
ordinary swans." And off they flew.

At first, Felix was so busy admiring his reflection that he

didn't really miss his friends. But, of course, it wasn't long before he started to feel very lonely. He hung his head and paddled sadly along the river.

The people who came down to the river couldn't help noticing that something was wrong. "Where have the other fine swans gone?" they asked. "There's only one sad-looking swan left."

After many days, Felix realised how silly he had been. He knew he had to do something, so he soared into the sky.

Over the countryside he flew, in search of his friends. At last he saw three beautiful swans swimming on a fine lake.

He swooped down shyly, afraid that they would send him away.

"I've missed you," he told them. "I'm sorry I was so vain and silly."

Of course, his friends didn't chase him away. They were delighted to see Felix. "We've missed you, too," they honked. "Why don't you stay with us ordinary swans?"

Felix was overjoyed. "I'd love to," he honked in reply, "but ... there is nothing ordinary about you!"

The Greedy Crows

It was milking time on Bluebell Farm and Farmer Jones was on his way to the cowshed. Mrs Jones, Farmer Jones's wife, came out of the farmhouse. She was wearing her smart clothes.

"I'm off to Sunnybridge market to do some shopping, Farmer Jones," she called to him. "Is there anything you need?"

"No, thanks!" said Farmer Jones. "You look very smart!"

"Thank you," said Mrs Jones. "You look like a scarecrow!"

"But I always dress like this," said Farmer Jones, looking down at his patched dungarees.

"That must be why you always look like a scarecrow," laughed Mrs Jones.

Later, Farmer Jones was in the milking parlour singing along to the radio when Max the sheepdog rushed in, barking.

"What is it?" asked Farmer Jones. As he followed Max out of the barn he could hear loud squawks coming from the cornfield. Farmer Jones began to run.

"Not those greedy crows again!" he cried. And, sure enough, a flock of crows was pecking away at Farmer Jones's lovely corn.

Farmer Jones raced around the field flapping his arms. But the crows just flew out of the way for a moment, then went back to their corn feast. "Can't catch us!" they cawed.

"I've got an idea!" said Farmer Jones suddenly.

"I know just what will get rid of those greedy crows!" And he ran off across the field and disappeared into his workshop. Soon the air was filled with a sound of hammering and sawing.

"Uh-oh!" said Pansy the pig. "It sounds like Farmer Jones is making something. And that usually means trouble."

Hours later, the workshop door swung open and a strange-looking machine rattled into sight.

"Introducing the Thingymajig!" cried Farmer Jones from behind the steering wheel.

The animals ran for cover as the Thingymajig crashed, banged and walloped its way towards the cornfield.

"Look out, you greedy crows!" chuckled Farmer Jones. "Here I come!"

He pulled a heavy lever and turned a huge dial. Out shot two tennis balls.

"Woof!" warned Max, as one tennis ball bounced on Pansy's bottom and landed in the water barrel. The second ball nearly hit the crows... but they just ducked.

"This isn't going to work!" thought Max.

"Take that!" Farmer Jones cried, fumbling with the lever. The Thingymajig began to rumble and rock. A spring flew into the air, spun around and knocked Farmer Jones into the duck pond. Then the Thingymajig collapsed into a heap.

"Caw! Caw! Caw!" laughed the crows.

Farmer Jones was soaked from head to toe. "It looks like I'll never get rid of those greedy crows," he said.

Back at the farmhouse, he emptied out his wellington boots, then took off his hat and dungarees. He was just hanging them on an old rake handle to dry when Mrs Jones arrived home.

"Oh dear!" she said.
"Whatever happened
to you?"

"It's a long story," said
Farmer Jones. "But the
long and short of it is I fell
into the duck pond."

"It's a good thing I bought you
these, then," smiled Mrs Jones. And she gave Farmer Jones a bag.
Inside were a new hat, shirt, dungarees and wellington boots.

Farmer Jones looked at his new clothes and looked at his old
clothes. Then he remembered what Mrs Jones had said that
morning. He grabbed both sets of clothes.

"I've got an idea!" he shouted.

Five minutes later, Farmer Jones came out of his workshop
carrying a scarecrow wearing his old clothes.

Max and Farmer Jones carried the scarecrow down to the
cornfield. The crows took one look at the scarecrow...

... and disappeared in fright!

Hector Protector

Hector Protector was dressed all in green;
Hector Protector was sent to the Queen.
The Queen did not like him,
No more did the King;
So Hector Protector
Was sent back again.

Higglety, Pigglety, Pop!

Higglety, pigglety, pop!
The dog has eaten the mop;
The pig's in a hurry,
The cat's in a flurry,
Higglety, pigglety, pop!

If Wishes Were Horses

If wishes were horses,
Beggars would ride;
If turnips were watches,
I'd wear one by my side.

Cushy Cow Bonny

Cushy cow bonny, let down thy milk,
And I will give thee a gown of silk;
A gown of silk and a silver tee,
If thou wilt let down thy milk for me.

There Was a Piper

There was a piper, he'd a cow,
And he'd no hay to give her;
He took his pipes and played a tune:
"Consider, old cow, consider!"
The cow considered very well,
For she gave the piper a penny,
That he might play the tune again,
Of, 'Corn rigs are bonnie'.

Tom, Tom, the Piper's Son

Tom, Tom, the piper's son,
Stole a pig, and away did run.
The pig was eat, and Tom was beat,
And Tom went roaring down the street.

The Bottom of the Sea

See, see, what can you see?
What can you see
At the bottom of the sea?
Shoals of fish that shimmer and shine,
Twisting, turning, all in time,
Yellow, red and stripy, too.
Fish of every shape and hue.
See, see, that's what you see.
That's what you see
At the bottom of the sea.

See, see, what can you see?
What can you see
At the bottom of the sea?
A coral reef far below,
Where pink anemones bloom and grow.
Crabs and starfish call it home,
And curious seahorses love to roam.
See, see, that's what you see.
That's what you see
At the bottom of the sea.

Surprise Sports Star

"Oh, no! We've got Jasmine," Jason whispered to Daniel and Sophie. "She's hopeless." The class was about to play basketball.

Sophie frowned. "Give Jasmine a chance," she said.

Staring at her shoes, Jasmine walked over to her team.

Miss Travers held up the basketball. "Ready?" she called. Then she blew her whistle.

During the game, Sophie saw Jasmine shy away whenever the ball came near.

But then, near the end of the game, Daniel yelled, "Jasmine! You're closest to the net!" He threw the ball towards her.

"Catch it!" yelled Jason.

Jasmine ran forward, holding out her arms.

Sophie held her breath.

The ball slipped through Jasmine's hands and bounced off the ground.

Sammy on the other team grabbed it and headed off to the other end of the court. He steered the ball up into the air and it dropped neatly into the net.

"Score!" his team shouted.

Miss Travers blew her

whistle. The game was over.

Sophie watched Jasmine trudge from the sports hall. She hurried to catch up with her. "Cheer up, Jasmine," she said. "It's supposed to be fun."

"I know," Jasmine replied quietly. "But I'm hopeless." She shrugged and walked away.

"Did you hear about the charity fun run?" Daniel asked Sophie as they walked home. "You collect sponsors and run laps around the school track."

Just then, Jasmine sprinted round the corner with her older brother. Both of them carried bags full of newspapers.

Sophie stopped, her eyes wide. "Look!" she said. "See how fast Jasmine's running!"

"Maybe she should enter the fun run," said Daniel.

Sophie nodded and began running after Jasmine. "Hey! Jasmine!" she called.

Jasmine stopped, allowing Sophie and Daniel to catch up.

"You're so fast!" Sophie panted.

Jasmine shrugged. "We run to get the paper round finished quickly," she said.

"Well, we think you should enter the fun run," Daniel said.

Now Jasmine looked surprised. "But I'm terrible at sports," she protested.

"You're not terrible at running, and that's a sport," Sophie pointed out.

Daniel patted Jasmine's paper bag. "Think about it," he said. "You're training every day, when you help your brother."

Jasmine shuffled her feet and looked down. "I'll think about it," she said.

On the morning of the fun run, Sophie and Daniel lined up with the other runners.

Daniel nudged Sophie. "Jasmine's here," he said, pointing to the other side of the crowd.

Sophie smiled. "Great!" she said. "I really hoped she would be."

"Ready, runners?" Miss Travers called. "You have one hour."

The starting whistle blew!

Sophie and Daniel began to run. A few seconds later, Jasmine sailed past.

After thirty minutes, at least half of the runners had dropped out. By fifty minutes, only a few were left running. And Jasmine was still out in front.

Miss Travers blew her whistle. "That's one hour!" she announced.

Jasmine came and sank onto the grass next to Sophie and Daniel. "You were right!" she beamed. "Running is a sport I can do well."

"Runners, gather around, please!" called Miss Travers. "You have all run like champions, "but the highest number of laps was run by… Jasmine!"

Everyone cheered and clapped. Miss Travers looked very pleased.

Jasmine looked very embarrassed.

"Well done!" whispered Sophie.

"And now that Jasmine has shown us what she can do, I hope she will join our cross-country running team," Miss Travers added.

Jasmine smiled with happiness. "Yes, please!" she said.

Car Wash Charlie

One sunny Saturday, Sam and his dad were washing the car.

"Woof!" barked Charlie the dog.

"I think Charlie wants to help, too," said Sam.

Dad looked at Charlie's muddy paws. "I'm not sure muddy dogs are very good at washing cars," he said. "But I guess he can watch."

The first thing Sam and his dad did was to splash water all over the car to get rid of the worst dirt. Charlie jumped around excitedly, chasing a blue butterfly.

Then Dad put some car soap in a bucket. "We need to go into the kitchen and fill this with water," he said.

When they came back, Dad looked at the car with a puzzled expression on his face.

"I was sure I'd rinsed that bit," he said, looking at a muddy smear on the side of the car and waving away the butterfly, which had settled on the wing mirror.

Sam and Dad got to work with their sponges, washing and rinsing the first side of the car. The soap made *loads* of bubbles! Charlie tried to eat some, but he didn't like the taste.

"Now the second side," said Dad. "But let's have a drink first."

In the kitchen, Dad had a cup of coffee and Sam had a glass of orange juice. Then they filled up their buckets and went back out to the car.

"Look, Sam," said Dad. "I think you missed a bit."

Sure enough, above the wheel was a muddy bit.

"Sorry, Dad," said Sam. But it was strange – he was sure he could remember washing that bit!

The two of them washed the other side of the car. The butterfly fluttered around Sam's head, while Charlie

nosed around in the puddles of water on the floor.

"Right!" said Dad, when they had finished. "Now we need to go and get some old towels from the garage to dry it with."

Sam and Dad went to the garage. "Can you stand on the chair and get the towels on that top shelf?" asked Dad.

Sam stood on the chair and stretched for the towels. Then, through the window he saw Charlie – jumping onto the bonnet of the freshly washed car in hot pursuit of the butterfly!

"Look, Dad!" cried Sam.

"*Charlie!*" shouted Dad, running out of the garage.

Charlie jumped off the bonnet. He looked very guilty.

Dad started to laugh. "I think we know now where those muddy smears came from," he said. "Time for you to go inside, Charlie. And after we've finished washing the car, our next job's going to be to wash *you*!"

Bunny Burrows

Little bunnies curled up tight,
Sleep in burrows through the night.
Cosy, warm and underground,
In the dark, there's not a sound.
There's just one thing I can't work out –
How do they know when the sun comes out?

Sammy Snail

Sammy Snail is slowly moving,
See him slide across the grass.
He leaves a silver path behind him,
We all know when he has passed.

Sammy Snail is never worried,
Though he wanders far and wide,
For on his back his house he carries,
And when he's tired he pops inside.

Don't Be Scared!

"Little Cub," said Dad, "I think the time's right
for you to come out with me to explore tonight."

Little Cub peered at the evening sky. The sun was slipping
down behind the trees. Shadows stretched across the plain.
As they set off, Little Cub shivered, and suddenly stopped.

"What's that high up there in that tree?"
he asked. "Two great big eyes watching me."

"Look closer, Little Cub. That thing up there
is just old Owl. Did he give you a scare?" asked Dad.

"Dad," smiled Little Cub, "Owl won't give me a scare.
He can't do that, as long as you're there."

Suddenly, Little Cub stopped. "What's that black shape

hanging down from that tree?
I felt it reaching out for me."

"Look closer, Little Cub.
That thing up there
is just old Snake. Did he give
you a scare?" asked Dad.

"Dad," smiled Little Cub,
"Snake won't give me a scare.
He can't do that, as long as
you're there."

Suddenly, Little Cub stopped.
"What's that I can hear
behind that tree?

There's a huge black
shadow following me."

"Look closer, Little Cub.

That thing back there is just old
Elephant. Did he give you a scare?" asked Dad.

"Dad," smiled Little Cub, "Elephant won't give me a scare.
He can't do that, as long as you're there."

Dad and Little Cub walked on. Suddenly, Dad stopped.

"What's that?" he asked.

"Toowhit, toowhoo! Ssss, ssss! Terummmp,
terummmp!"

The animals jumped out at Dad. Dad jumped!

"Don't be scared," laughed Little Cub.

"Sorry, Lion! Did we give you a scare?" asked the animals,
laughing.

"No!" said Dad. "You couldn't give me a scare.
Not as long as Little Cub is there."

Then, side by side, Little Cub and Dad headed for home.

Take the Ghost Train

There's a tumbledown old station,
Where a ghost train waits to go.
All aboard, ghosts, ghouls and goblins,
Watch the engine brightly glow!

Ghostly guards are whistling wildly,
Bony fingers wave goodbye,
As along the rails the ghost train glides,
Beneath the moonlit sky.

Witches shriek along the railcars,
While inside the dining car,
Vampires munch and crunch with monsters
Sipping cocktails at the bar!

If there were tickets for the ghost train,
Would you dare to take a ride?
Or would you quickly run away,
And find somewhere to hide?

Ode to Ghosts

A ghost he has a sad old life
Haunting empty castles.
On birthdays and at Christmas time
The postman brings no parcels.

He floats around from room to room,
He howls and clanks his chains.
But everyone ignores the noise,
And blames it on the drains.

And if by chance he should appear
Most people scream with fright.
He just can't understand it –
Is he such a dreadful sight?

So if you ever meet a ghost
Don't run away in fright.
Stay awhile and have a chat,
You'll find they're most polite.

Tia and Teddy

Tia's Mouse's favourite toy was Teddy.

Teddy went with Tia everywhere. When Teddy was with Tia, Tia wasn't scared of anything. She wasn't scared of climbing to the top of the stalks of corn in the field nearby, or bigger mice, or doing somersaults, or anything at all.

"You and Teddy are so brave!" Mum would say, as Tia told her about another one of their adventures together.

One afternoon, though, Tia looked all through the mouse hole, but she couldn't find Teddy anywhere.

Tia started to cry. "Mum! Teddy's gone missing!"

Mum came out of the study. "I'm sure he's somewhere, Tia," she said. "Don't worry, we'll find him."

"I'm scared without Teddy," said Tia.

Tia and Mum went to look for Teddy. They looked in the corn field. Then they looked down by the stream. And there was Teddy! He was propped up against a tree.

"We were looking at the fish this morning with Dad," said Tia. "Teddy must have decided to watch them for a bit longer."

"Well he's found now," said Mum, giving them both a big hug.

That night Tia couldn't sleep. She lay awake and looked at the dark. Suddenly she felt scared of the shadows. She crept out of bed and went into her mum's room.

"I'm scared, Mum," said Tia.

"But you're never scared when you're with Teddy," said Mum.

"But what if I lose him again?" said Tia.

Mum smiled. "Let me tell you a secret," she said. "Do you know what Teddy said to me when we came back from the stream this morning? He told me that he was scared when he was on his own by the stream, but he's never scared when he's with you, because you're so brave."

"So I think Teddy's the brave one," said Tia...

"... but he thinks you are!" finished Mum.

"Perhaps we're both brave." said Tia. "Do you know, I think I might be ready to go back to bed now." She gave Mum a big hug, and Mum hugged her and Teddy back.

"Night, night, Tia. Night, night, Teddy," said Mum.

"Night, night, Mum," said Tia. "Teddy says 'night night' as well. And he says to tell you he's not scared any more."

Kiera the Kite

It was a dark and stormy night, and Kiera the kite was one of the few creatures who dared to go out. She had a chick to feed and had left her mountaintop nest to hunt.

At last Kiera managed to snare a juicy mouse and set off for home. She flapped her powerful wings and battled against the wind. The wind was so strong that she couldn't fly very fast. It was almost dawn when she finally spotted her nest. She swooped down in triumph, and then shuddered to a halt.

"**Squawk!**" she cried. Her nest was empty! Where was her baby? Kiera hopped around in alarm. She didn't know what to do. Then she had an idea. She flapped her wings and soared high into the sky. Hovering above the ground, she scanned the area with her sharp eyes. Almost immediately she spotted a movement far below and swooped down. Kiera screeched with joy. There was her little chick, sitting safely on a rocky ledge.

"I'm okay," squeaked the little chick. "I jumped out of the nest because it was swaying in the wind."

"I think it's time to teach you how to fly," smiled Kiera.

A New Pool for Otter

Otter had lived in the animal sanctuary for as long as he could remember. Then, one day, his keeper lifted him out of his pen and placed him in a crate. Otter was so scared that he couldn't move. He curled into a ball and shook with fright as the lid closed and everything went dark.

"What's happening?" he wondered.

Otter felt himself being carried along and put down. Then a door slammed, and an engine roared into life. The engine purred as Otter bumped gently around in his crate. Finally the engine stopped and the door was opened.

Otter's crate was lifted out and placed on to the ground. Sunlight flooded in as the lid opened. Otter blinked and sniffed the air. He looked around before creeping out. Suddenly, he was bursting with happiness. There in front of him was a woodland pool, twinkling in the sun.

"Welcome home!" smiled his keeper. SPLASH! Otter dived into the crystal-clear water and darted after the fish. He was free…

The Little Turtle

There was a little turtle,
He lived in a box,
He swam in a puddle,
He climbed on the rocks.
He snapped at a mosquito,
He snapped at a flea,
He snapped at a minnow,
And he snapped at me.
He caught the mosquito,
He caught the flea,
He caught the minnow,
But he didn't catch me!

Tiny Tim

There was a little turtle,
His name was Tiny Tim.
I put him in the bathtub,
To see if he could swim.
He drank up all the water,
He ate up all the soap,
And now he is in the bathtub,
With a bubble in his throat.
Bubble, bubble, bubble,
Bubble, bubble, pop!

The Three Little Pigs

Once upon a time there were three little pigs. One day the three little pigs set off to find new homes.

Soon the three little pigs saw a pile of straw.

"I'll build my house of straw," said the first little pig.

The two little pigs walked on. They saw a big pile of sticks underneath an oak tree.

"I'll build my house of sticks," said the second pig.

The third little pig walked on. He saw a pile of bricks.

"I'll build a strong house of bricks," said the third little pig.

It took the third little pig a long time to build his house. His brothers laughed at him for working so hard. But the house of bricks was very strong.

The very next day, a big bad wolf called at the house of straw.

"Little pig, little pig, let me come in," said the wolf.

"Not by the hair of my chinny chin chin!" said the first little pig. So the wolf huffed and he puffed and he blew the house down.

The little pig ran away

and hid with his brother in the house of sticks.

The next day, the big bad wolf called at the house of sticks.

"Little pig, little pig, let me come in," he said.

"Not by the hair of my chinny chin chin!" said the second little pig. So the wolf huffed and he puffed and he blew the house down.

The two little pigs ran away and hid with their brother in the house of bricks.

The next day, the big bad wolf called at the house of bricks.

"Little pig, little pig, let me come in," said the wolf.

"Not by the hair of my chinny chin chin!" said the third little pig. So the wolf huffed and he puffed. But he couldn't blow the house down.

The big bad wolf was very cross. "I'm coming down the chimney to eat you!" he cried.

The third little pig made a fire under the chimney. Then he put a pot of water on the fire.

The big bad wolf climbed down the chimney and *Splash!* He fell into the pot of hot water.

"Help! Help!" cried the wolf. He jumped out of the pot and ran out of the house.

And he was never seen again.

My Pigeon House

My pigeon house I open wide,
To set my pigeons free.
They fly around and up and down,
And land in the tallest tree.
And when they return from their merry flight,
They close their eyes and say good night.
Coo-coo-coo! Good night!

Cock-a-doodle-doo!

Cock-a-doodle-doo!
My dame has lost her shoe;
My master's lost his fiddling-stick,
And doesn't know what to do.

Cock-a-doodle-doo!
What is my dame to do?
Till master finds his fiddling-stick,
She'll dance without her shoe.

Cock-a-doodle-doo!
My dame has found her shoe,
And master's found his fiddling-stick;
Sing cock-a-doodle-doo!

Mabel Gets Lost

One sunny day, Mrs Duck took her ducklings for a swim.

"Whatever you do, stay close, and don't wander off," she warned her brood.

But Mabel, the smallest duckling, wasn't listening. She was too busy chasing butterflies. Mabel waddled along behind a colourful butterfly until it disappeared across the river. Then she looked around. She  had wandered a long way from home, and had never seen this part of the river before. But Mabel didn't mind. There were lots of interesting things to see. She watched a blue kingfisher diving for fish. Then she saw some otters playing on the bank. Above, a flock of swans soared across the sky.

"Quack, quack!" she cried. "This is an exciting place!"

She called out to the otters, but they were too busy messing around to hear her. Suddenly, Mabel began to miss her mum and her brothers and sisters.

"I'd better go home," she quacked. But when she looked around, Mabel didn't know which way to go.

"Oh, no," she wailed. "I'm lost." And she sat down beside

the river to cry. She had been crying for a few minutes when the water in front her began to ripple. Then two bulging eyes, followed by a green head, popped up. It was her friend Herbert the frog. Mabel gulped and tried to wipe away her tears.

"What's wrong?" Herbert asked kindly.

"I'm lost," wept Mabel. "And I miss my mum."

"Don't worry," croaked Herbert. "Jump into the river and swim behind me. I'll show you the way home."

So Mabel followed Herbert downstream until they bumped into Mrs Duck and the other ducklings.

"Hooray! I'm home at last!" quacked Mabel, leaping out of the water and rushing to her mum's side.

Mrs Duck was so pleased to see her that she forgot to be angry.

"I'll stay close to you from now on," quacked Mabel.

Curious Kitten

Snowball was a very curious kitten. One day, she watched Mrs Duck lead her ducklings across the yard. They looked so funny waddling along that Snowball decided to join them.

"I wonder what it's like being a duck," she thought. She scurried along behind the ducklings, trying her best to quack – but all she could manage was a strange "Meeaak!"

Snowball watched as the ducklings nibbled the grass on the riverbank. She tried a little herself, but it made her cough. Then she watched as the ducklings followed their mother into the water.

"Swimming looks easy," she thought, so she jumped in. SPLASH! Of course, Snowball quickly discovered that swimming wasn't easy for a kitten at all.

"Help!" she spluttered, as she tried to keep her head above water.

Luckily, Tank the sheepdog was nearby. He leaped in and pulled her out before she could come to any harm.

Once Snowball had recovered, she crept back into the house and lay in front of the warm fire.

"I'd far rather be a kitten than a duck," she purred.

Shy Octopus

Harry was a shy octopus who lived in a quiet corner of the coral reef. He rarely came out and if he bumped into anyone, he would squeeze himself into the nearest crack and hide – because, being a rubbery octopus, he could squeeze himself into places that no one else could reach.

One day, Harry was hiding when he heard a shout.

"Help!" cried a tiny voice. "It's me, Crab! I've fallen down a crack and I can't get out."

Harry peered out of his hidey-hole and watched as the other sea creatures did their best to rescue their friend.

First Seahorse tried to squeeze into the crack… then Angelfish… and finally Eel. But it was no use. They were all far too big. Harry knew that he would have to help, so he coughed shyly.

"Allow me," he said. And much to everyone's surprise, he squeezed his rubbery body into the crack and used a long tentacle to pull the tiny crab free. Everyone cheered.

"My hero!" sighed the tiny crab, smiling at Harry.

Harry blushed but felt very pleased. Maybe making friends wasn't going to be so difficult after all.

Super Snakes

One day Seymour Snake's cousin, Sadie, came to stay.

"Sadie!" cried Seymour. "It's so good to see you! Come and meet my friends! You can play games with us, and –"

"Oh, I don't play games any more," Sadie interrupted. "I've been going to Madame Sylvia's Snake School. Madame Sylvia always says, 'A well-behaved snake may slither and glide and wriggle and slide, but we *don't* swing or sway, or climb or play!'"

"Well, will you come and meet my friends?" Seymour asked.

"Oh, yesss," hissed Sadie. "It would be rude not to!"

"Hey, Seymour!" shouted Maxine Monkey. "Come and play Coconut Catch with Mickey and me!"

"You can come and play, too," Seymour said to Sadie.

"No, thank you," said Sadie. "I'll just watch."

Seymour spent hours hanging and swinging and climbing. Each time, Seymour invited Sadie to join him. But Sadie always said, "I mustn't swing or sway, or climb or play."

Suddenly, Seymour had an idea.

The next day, Sadie was gliding through the jungle when she found Ellen and Emma Elephant, staring up into a tree.

"What's going on?" Sadie asked.

"We were playing Fling the Melon," said Ellen, "and the melon got stuck in that tree. We can't reach it!"

"Oh, dear," said Sadie. "I'm sure Seymour will be happy to climb up and get it for you."

But Seymour had disappeared!

"Can't you help us, Sadie?" Emma asked. "We know about Madame Sylvia's rules. But surely Madame Sylvia must have taught you that it's important to help others."

"Yes, she did," said Sadie. So up she went, winding her way up the trunk and into the branches. She found the melon and gave it a shove. It fell down into Ellen's waiting trunk.

"Thanks, Sadie!" said Emma. "Are you coming down now?"

"Er, not just yet," said Sadie. "I just want to try something first." With a quick wriggle, Sadie coiled herself round the branch and hung upside down above the elephants.

"This is *sssstupendous!*" Sadie hissed. She swung herself over to another tree. "*Wheee!*" she cried.

"I knew you'd like swinging and climbing if you gave it a try," called Seymour, coming out from where he'd been hiding.

"Come up here, Seymour!" Sadie called.

"But what will you tell Madame Sylvia?" asked Seymour.

"I'll just tell her," said Sadie, "that we *must* climb and play, and swing and sway – *all day!*"

Howls and Owls

"*Owwww!*" A horrible howl rang out through the darkness. Beneath the moon, Hairy the Horrible Hound sat staring at his paws.

He had been howling away all evening. He wanted someone to talk to, someone to play with. But because he was a ghost hound no one would come near.

The moon shone between the clouds and lit up the ruined manor house on top of the hill. The people who once lived there had fled years ago. Now it was just the haunt of Shiver, an old ghost.

Shiver was resting. At the first sound of Hairy's howls, he groaned. "Hairy's dreadful noise goes right through my skull!" he cried. "Something must be done!"

"Who's Hairy?" a voice above Shiver asked. An owl flitted through a hole in the roof.

"Hairy is the ghost hound who howls horribly outside in the lane," said Shiver. "I wish he would stop."

"He might, if you ask him nicely," blinked the owl.

"M-me? Face Hairy the Horrible Hound?" breathed Shiver.

"Well, someone should!" said the

owl. "I only flew in yesterday and I must say, I'm tired of that howling already! I suppose I'll have to do it myself."

Soon the owl was back. But this time he wasn't alone! There was a padding of paws on the front steps, then the door swung open on its creaky hinges.

"Yikes! Time I disappeared!" trembled Shiver. But it was too late! In swept the owl, followed by the ghostly hound.

"Hairy told me he only howls because he's lonely," said the owl. "He chases anything that moves, too, in the hope of finding a friend! If you want my advice, you should let him come and live here. What better than a ghostly guard dog?"

"I promise I'd never howl again," pleaded Hairy, hopefully.

"You can lie beside my old bed, Hairy," smiled Shiver, who wasn't the least bit nervous now.

And so Hairy the Horrible Hound found a home at last.

But if Shiver had hoped for some peace and quiet, he was to be sadly disappointed. For if Hairy wasn't playfully pulling the sheets off Shiver, he was leaping onto his lap for company.

Slowly, though, Shiver grew to like things being more lively. Which was just as well, or Hairy might have had to start howling again!

King of the Castle

Ross and Jane were exploring an old castle near the campsite they were staying on. They saw someone they knew.

"Oh no, it's Sam," said Ross. Sam was climbing a wall.

Jane pointed to the big sign. It said *Danger*!

"Come down!" said Jane.

"You will fall!" said Ross. But Sam carried on climbing. He stood on top of the wall. He marched up and down. "I'm the king of the castle!" he said.

"Look!" said Ross. "The wall is falling down."

"Sam, you are in danger!" said Jane.

Bang! A few bricks fell off the top of the wall.

"Watch out, Sam!" cried Jane.

"Don't be such a scaredy-cat!" shouted Sam, scornfully.

Crash! A whole section of the wall fell down. Sam slipped...

"*Sam!*" shouted Ross.

Sam just managed to hold on to the top of the wall with his fingertips. "Help me!" he shouted. "Help me! I'm about to fall!"

"Hold on!" said Ross.

Ross and Jane ran back to the campsite to get help.

Soon a fire engine arrived. The firemen put a ladder against the wall and lifted Sam down.

"Thank goodness you're safe," said Sam's mum, giving him a big hug.

"Don't do that again," said the fireman, sternly.

"I won't," said Sam. "Thank you for saving me."

And for once it looked as though Sam might mean it!

ABC

ABC,
Our kitty's up the tree!
And now begins,
With a sneeze and a cough,
To lick her long white stockings off.
No more she'll go into the snow.
Not she, not she, not she!

Magpie

One for sorrow.
Two for joy.
Three for a girl.
Four for a boy.
Five for silver.
Six for gold.
Seven for a secret
Never to be told.
Eight's a wish.
Nine's a kiss.
Ten is a bird you
Must not miss!
Magpie!

One Dark Night

Paws tiptoed out into the dark farmyard.
Mummy had told him to stay in the barn
until he was old enough to go out at night,
but he was impatient.

"*Toowhit, toowhoo!*" A loud hoot echoed
through the trees, and a great dark shape
swooped down and snatched something
up.

"Just an owl," Paws told himself,
creeping nervously on into the darkness.
"Nothing to be afraid of!"

Strange rustlings came from every corner.

Grunt! Paws jumped. But it was just the old
pig in the pigsty close by.

Then, all of a sudden, Paws froze in his tracks. Beneath
the hen house two eyes glinted in the darkness. They came
creeping towards him… this must be the fox
Mummy had warned him about! But
then, to his amazement, he saw it was
Mummy!

"Back to the barn!" she said
sternly. And Paws happily did as
he was told. Maybe he would wait
until he was older to go out at night,
after all!

The Dotty Professor

Professor Von Bean was very excited. He had finished
building his machine and it was ready to use. It was the most
complicated contraption he had ever built.

The professor called his assistant to come to watch him start
the machine. The wheels were green and brown, and there
were levers on either side. The side panels were striped red and
white, and there was a big chimney on the top for the smoke to
escape. There was a cupboard on the side which, the professor
explained, was to hang a wet coat in. There was a shelf on the
back for a box of plants.

While Professor Von Bean was getting more and more
excited, his assistant looked very worried.

"But what does it do?" he asked, timidly.

The professor scratched his head and thought.

"Oh dear, oh dear!" he sighed. "What a fool
I have been! Why didn't I think of that? It
does absolutely nothing useful at all!"

Little Dragon

Little Dragon was reading a book all about a nasty man in a tin suit who bashes up poor little dragons. Little Dragon felt all worried and wobbly. Just then, Little Dragon heard voices.

"Oh, no!" thought Little Dragon. "Dragon-bashers!" And he hid under his blanket.

Outside, Princess Pippa, Prince Pip and Little Baron Boris were walking up the hill. Boris was making a lot of noise and waving a toy sword.

"Let's go on a dragon hunt," said Boris. "Are you coming?"

"No, thank you," said Pippa and Pip.

"Scaredy cats, scaredy cats!" sang Boris.

"We are not scaredy cats!" said Pip angrily.

"Look!" cried Boris. "Dragon footprints!"

They followed the footprints right up to Little Dragon's door.

"Er ... you two go first," said Boris. "I'll stand outside and guard the door in case the dragon tries to escape."

Pip and Pippa pushed the door open. It was very dark and spooky inside the cave. They saw a light, and a big shadow that looked like ... a dragon! They were very frightened!

"Who's there?" asked Pip bravely.

"It's me!" said Little Dragon.

"Are you a dragon?" asked Pippa.

"Yes," said Little Dragon.

"You're very small," said Pippa.

"I'm big on the inside," said Little Dragon, standing on tippy toes. Then he started to cry. "Are you going to bash me up now, like in my book?" he sniffed.

"Of course not," said Pippa, and she gave him a big hug.

"Let's just be friends," said Prince Pip. So that was settled.

"Would you like a snack?" asked Little Dragon.

"Oh, yes, please!" said Pippa and Pip. Little Dragon fetched a plate of jam doughnuts.

"Does your noisy friend with the pointy stick want one?" asked Little Dragon.

"Oh, you mean Boris," said Pippa. "I'm sure he'd like one. He's always hungry!"

"Would you like a doughnut, Boris?" asked Little Dragon.

"It's a dragon!" cried Little Baron Boris.

"Now who's a scaredy cat?" laughed Pip.

Soon it was time for Pip and Pippa to go.

"Can we be friends tomorrow?" asked Little Dragon.

"We'll be friends forever,"
said Pip and Pippa.

I Love You, Grandpa

Little Bear and Grandpa were walking by the river when Little Bear spotted a fish darting through the water.

"Quick, Grandpa!" he yelled. He rushed into the river, caught the fish, and held it up proudly for Grandpa to see.

Grandpa smiled. "My legs were once strong and speedy like yours," he said. "But now I've found an easier way to catch a meal."

"Really, Grandpa?" asked Little Bear. "What's that?"

"Well," replied Grandpa, "I'm more crafty now. I stand here at the rapids and I wait until the fish jump out of the water... straight into my mouth."

"Wow!" said Little Bear. "I love you, Grandpa. You're so clever!"

Just then, Eagle swooped down. The beat of his wings ruffled the bears' fur. They saw his sharp claws.

Little Bear ran straight up a tree. Grandpa smiled.

"I can remember when I could climb as well as you," he said. "But now I don't need to run away."

"Really, Grandpa?" asked Little Bear. "What do you do?"

"Well," replied Grandpa, "I'm bolder now." When Eagle swooped again, Grandpa barked in his deep, gruff voice. He roared, and Eagle swerved away over the mountains.

"Wow!" said Little Bear. "I love you, Grandpa. You're so brave!"

They walked on until they came across a slope where the earth was softer and deeper.

"Watch me, Grandpa!" called Little Bear. "I can dig myself a really good hollow to sleep in through the winter."

Grandpa smiled. "I can remember when I could dig as well as you," he sighed. "But now I know a better way to find a hollow."

"Really, Grandpa?" frowned Little Bear. "But where do you spend the winter?"

"Well," replied Grandpa, "I'm wiser now. All I need to do is to find a hollow tree. Follow me." And he led Little Bear to a huge tree.

In the middle of its massive trunk was a snug hollow.

"I love you, Grandpa," said Little Bear. "You know so much. Will I ever be as crafty, brave and wise as you?"

"Of course you will!" replied Grandpa.

Soon soft flakes of snow began to fall. Inside the hollow, Little Bear snuggled up to Grandpa.

"I love you, Grandpa," he said again.

Grandpa ruffled Little Bear's messy head. "I love you too, Little Bear," Grandpa said.

The Fairy Ball

Late at night when the moon is bright,
And the air is soft and still,
Pixies peep and fairies creep,
And goblins roam at will.

Elves sneak out, and slink about,
Leprechauns come leaping.
Little sprites wave magic lights,
While the world is sleeping.

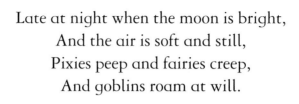

Singing songs, they skip along,
Towards the forest glade.
Hung with lights, all twinkling bright,
While gentle music's played.

They appear, from far and near,
A host of fairy folk.
This happy band dance hand in hand,
Beneath the magic oak.

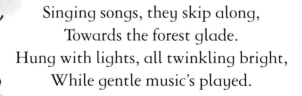

Where Lies the Land?

Where lies the land to which the ship would go?
Far, far ahead, is all her seamen know.
And where the land she travels from? Away,
Far, far behind, is all that they can say.
On sunny noons upon the deck's smooth face,
Linked arm in arm, how pleasant here to pace;
Or, o'er the stern reclining, watch below
The foaming wake far widening as we go.

On stormy nights when wild north-westers rave,
How proud a thing to fight with wind and wave!
The dripping sailor on the reeling mast
Exults to bear, and scorns to wish it past.
Where lies the land to which the ship would go?
Far, far ahead, is all her seamen know.
And where the land she travels from? Away,
Far, far behind, is all that they can say.

Brother and Sister

"*Sister*, sister, go to bed!
Go and rest your weary head."
Thus the prudent brother said.

"Do you want a battered hide,
Or scratches to your face applied?"
Thus his sister calm replied.

"Sister, do not raise my wrath.
I'd make you into mutton broth
As easily as kill a moth!"

The sister raised her beaming eye
And looked on him indignantly
And sternly answered, "Only try!"

Off to the cook he quickly ran.
"Dear Cook, please lend a frying-pan
To me as quickly as you can."

"And wherefore should I lend it you?"
"The reason, Cook, is plain to view.
I wish to make an Irish stew."

"What meat is in that stew to go?"
"My sister'll be the contents!" "Oh!"
"You'll lend the pan to me, Cook?" "No!"

Moral: Never stew your sister.

The Crow and the Pitcher

One hot summer day, when there had been no rain for months and all the ponds and rivers had dried up, a thirsty crow was searching for a drink. At last he spotted a pitcher of cool water in a garden, and flew down to take a drink. But when he put his head into the neck of the pitcher, it was only half full, and the crow could not reach the water.

Now, the crow was a smart bird, so he came up with a plan — he would break the neck of the pitcher, then reach down to the water below.

Tap! Tap! Tap! The crow pecked the pitcher with his sharp beak again and again, but it was so hard and strong, he couldn't make even the tiniest crack.

The crow did not give up easily, so he thought of another plan. He would tip the pitcher over. The bird pushed and pushed as hard as he could, but the pitcher was very heavy, and it would not move at all.

The poor crow knew that if he did not get a drink soon he would die of thirst. He had to find some way of getting to the water in the pitcher! As he looked around, wondering what to do, he saw some pebbles on the path, and he had an idea.

He picked up a pebble in his beak and dropped it into the pitcher. The water level rose a little. The bird got another pebble and dropped it in. The water rose a little more. The crow worked very hard, dropping more and more pebbles into the pitcher until the water was almost at the top.

At last the bird was able to reach the water – and he drank and drank until he could drink no more. His clever idea had saved his life.

Aesop's moral:
Little by little
does the trick.

The Ant and the Dove

One morning, a thirsty ant crawled down to the edge of a river to take a drink. As he was quenching his thirst, a boat passed by, making waves. SWOOSH! The waves swept the poor ant into the water and carried him downstream.

Luckily, a kind dove sitting in a tree on the riverbank saw what was happening. Quick as a flash, she dropped a leaf into the water near the ant, who was able to climb on to it and float back to the shore.

A little later, the ant was drying off in the sun when he saw a bird-catcher heading for the river with his net. Very slowly, the man crept up to the tree where the dove was sitting and quietly laid out his net to trap her. The ant was determined to help the kind creature who had saved his life, so he opened his jaws and bit the bird-catcher on the foot.

"Ouch!" yelled the man loudly. Startled by the loud noise, the dove flew away, and was saved from the bird-catcher's net!

Aesop's moral:
One good turn
deserves another.

The Thrush

It was winter, and Tufty the thrush's garden home
was full of joy. There were juicy worms to eat and
five lively children to watch as they played in
the snow. She even enjoyed the games
of chase she played with the
cat next door.

But when spring arrived,
Tufty realised that she needed
somewhere quiet to build her
nest – somewhere peaceful and
safe, away from the playful cat.
Tufty searched until she found
the perfect place in an old teapot on a shelf in the shed.

One day, the children banged into the shed in search
of a ball. The tallest boy saw the nest right away.

"Ooooh! Our thrush has made a nest," he said. "Let's leave
her alone and close the door so that Kitty can't get in."

A few days later the eggs hatched, and Tufty had five
perfect babies of her own. It wasn't long before they were ready
to make their first trip into the garden.

One by one, Tufty led her brood outside to munch on juicy
worms and watch the children play.

"Look at our thrush's new family!" cried the
children. "Aren't they the prettiest chicks you have ever seen!"

Tufty was so proud, she sang her heart out!

How the Bear Lost His Tail

Once upon a time, the bear had a long, black, glossy tail, and the fox was very jealous of it.

"What makes Bear think his tail is so wonderful?" growled the fox to himself. "My tail is much finer than his. I'm going to teach him a lesson."

It was winter, and all the lakes were covered with thick ice. The fox made a hole in the ice and surrounded it with fat, tasty-looking fish. That evening, when the bear passed by, the fox dangled his tail through the hole into the water.

"What are you doing?" the bear asked.

"I am fishing," the fox replied. "Would you like to try?"

The bear loved to eat fish, so he was very eager to try.

"As you can see, I have caught all the fish in this spot," the fox told him. "Let's go over there and make a new hole."

They walked over to a shallow part of the lake, and the fox

cut a hole in the ice.

"This is what you must do," the fox explained. "Turn your back to the hole and don't think about fish at all – otherwise they will sense that you are trying to catch them and they won't come near. Soon a fish will grab your tail, then you can pull it out. In the meantime you must be very patient and stay perfectly still."

The bear put his long tail through the hole in the ice and did exactly as the fox had told him.

The next morning, the fox went back to the lake and saw that the bear was still sitting on the ice. He was fast asleep and covered in snow. The hole had frozen over during the night and now the bear's tail was trapped in the ice.

"You've caught a fish! Pull out your tail!" cried the fox.

The bear woke up with a start and tugged his tail as hard as he could. All of a sudden, there was a loud CRACK! as the bear's frozen tail snapped off.

And that explains why bears have very short tails and why they are definitely not friends with foxes.

Gilbert's Umbrella

One day, Gilbert the mouse was out walking when it started to rain. At first, it was just the occasional drop – pitter patter – but then it began to pour. So Gilbert put up his umbrella and hurried towards his home in the Old Oak Tree.

When he was almost there, Gilbert noticed something very worrying. A river of rain was gushing down the hill – and his cosy, dry home in the Old Oak Tree was on the other side. Before he could decide what to do, a gust of wind blew his umbrella into the water.

"That's it!" cried Gilbert, "I'll use my umbrella as a boat!" Gilbert leaped in and – SWOOSH! – he was swept away. "Oh dear!" he cried. "How can I make it stop?"

The rain river swept Gilbert along, until BUMP – his boat came to a halt. Gilbert laughed. The umbrella had bumped into the roots of the Old Oak Tree. He was home!

"That was fun!" he squeaked as he scrambled out, "but I think I'll stick to walking from now on."

Prudence Stays Up

Prudence the kitten was very excited. Mummy had promised to take her hunting by the light of the moon. "I can't wait! I can't wait!" meowed Prudence, running around in circles.

"You can only go if you have a nap this afternoon," warned Mummy Cat. "Otherwise you'll be too tired."

But Prudence was much too excited to take a nap. As soon as her mother had gone she padded around the farm to tell all her friends.

"I'm a big girl now!" she boasted. "I'll be out until dawn."

By dusk everyone knew about the hunting trip, but Prudence was nowhere to be found. "Where can she be?" called Mummy Cat. Suddenly she heard a loud snoring sound coming from high up in a tree. She looked up, and there was Prudence, fast asleep. All the excitement had worn her out. There would be no night hunting for Prudence tonight.

"Never mind," smiled Mummy Cat. "There's always tomorrow!"

Who Lives in a Hole?

Who lives in the hole in the wall of my house?
Can you guess – it's a little brown mouse!

A Swarm of Bees in May

A swarm of bees in May is worth a load of hay.
A swarm of bees in June is worth a silver spoon.
A swarm of bees in July isn't worth a fly.

Old Farmer Giles

Old Farmer Giles,
He went seven miles
With his faithful dog Old Rover;
And his faithful dog Old Rover,
When he came to the stiles,
Took a run and jumped clean over.

If Pigs Could Fly

If pigs could fly
High in the sky,
Where do you think they'd go?
Would they follow a plane
To France or Spain,
Or drift where the wind blows?

There Was an Old Lady

There was an old lady who swallowed a fly,
I don't know why she swallowed a fly.
Perhaps she'll die!

There Was Once a Fish

There was once a fish. (What more could you wish?)
He lived in the sea. (Where else would he be?)
He was caught on a line. (Whose line if not mine?)
So I brought him to you. (What else should I do?)

Monster Mash

Beware the monster mash!
'Cause monsters cook up trash,
Spaghetti hoops with liquorice loops –
They'll give you a nasty rash!

Beware the monster brew!
It's a grim and gristly stew,
Of turnip tops and vile black drops –
Better flush it down the loo!

Beware the monster drink!
It's lime green, mauve and pink,
And made with peas and dead gnats' knees –
It's bound to cause a stink!

Beware the monster gruel!
It's only good for fuel,
Brown rats' tails and slugs and snails –
To eat it would be cruel!

Beware the monster sweets!
They're made of dragons' feet,
With sugared claws and chocolate paws –
They're gruesome, not a treat!

Beware the monster snack!
It's bubbling puce and black,
It's made from tar and bits of car –
So quickly hand it back!

Beware the monster bill,
They're adding at the till,
If the food's not enough to make you rough –
The cost will make you ill!

The Cowardly Lion

Once upon a time there was a lion called Sabre. Sabre looked just like other lions. He had a big shaggy mane, huge powerful claws, and teeth like daggers. And just like other lions, the whole jungle rumbled when he roared. But Sabre wasn't actually like other lions at all. He wasn't fierce and scary – he was a cowardly lion. When other animals challenged him to a fight, he simply fiddled with his tail and looked silly. Even the dogs from the nearby village laughed at him.

Poor old Sabre felt very lonely.

Then one day, as Sabre was walking through the jungle, a terrible thing happened. Something flickered in the undergrowth and then flames began to leap out of the trees. A herd of elephants charged past, heading for the safety of the watering hole. More and more animals joined the stampede. Only Sabre and one of the dogs from the village stayed where they were.

"Help," barked the dog. "My puppy is back there in the fire."

Sabre didn't wait to hear more. He gave a great ROAR
and leaped into the flames. Moments later, he was back
holding a small black bundle in his gentle jaws. He dropped
the puppy beside its mother and raced down to the waterhole.
But he didn't stay long. He gulped
down a mouthful of water
and rushed back to the
flames.

All the other animals watched in amazement as Sabre spat the
water into the fire. What was he doing?

Suddenly, the elephants realised what he was trying to do.
Sabre was trying to put out the fire. He was trying to save
the jungle!

One by one, the elephants joined in, using their trunks to
squirt water at the flames. Before long, the fire was out.
Thanks to Sabre, the puppy and the jungle had been saved.

At long last, the other animals realised that Sabre wasn't a
cowardly lion after all. He was a very brave lion. A very brave
lion, who just didn't like fighting!

The Science Project

Jed's mum was on the phone. Jed sat at the top of the stairs, listening carefully.

"Mission understood, sir," said Mum. "You can rely on me." She put down the phone and went into the kitchen to finish making dinner.

Jed crept into Mum's office. She had left her work on the computer screen. It told him all about her new mission. Jed smiled.

"Looks like we're going to be busy," he said quietly.

Mum tried to keep her job a secret from Jed, but he knew she was a special agent. A spy! She worked for Unit X, a top-secret organization used by the government to sort out its trickiest problems.

Jed had a secret of his own: he sometimes helped Mum on her missions. But he made sure she never found out.

Jed looked at the computer screen and read about the new mission. An important new invention had gone missing: a new energy-saving fuel. Mum had to find it and return it to the Winger Science Centre – as soon as possible!

"Dinner's ready, Jed!" Mum called.

Jed turned away from the computer and went downstairs.

"Your favourite!" said Mum, passing him a plateful of chicken curry. "Have you got any homework this weekend?" she asked.

Suddenly, Jed had an idea. "I have a science project on pollution," he replied. "My teacher said the Winger Science Centre has a good exhibition. Can we go there, please?" Jed held his breath. Would Mum take the bait?

Mum looked surprised. "What a coincidence!" she said. "I have to visit the Winger Science Centre tomorrow afternoon. You can come with me."

The next afternoon, Mum pulled into the Winger Science Centre car park. "I'll go and talk to the manager while you look at the exhibition," she said. "Meet you in an hour."

"OK," Jed replied. But as Mum walked away, Jed ran off around the side of the building.

Seeing an open window on the ground floor, Jed climbed through it. He found himself in a long corridor. Suddenly he heard a familiar voice. Mum!

Jed quickly hid behind a big pot plant as Mum turned the corner, talking to the research centre manager.

"Here's my office," said the manager, opening a door.

Jed breathed a sigh of relief as they disappeared inside.

Mum hadn't seen anything.

Then Jed heard another voice.

"Here, Puss!" it called, from a nearby room.

A large cat hurried past. Jed followed it to a boiler room.

Inside the boiler room, an old caretaker was putting cat food into a bowl. Jed watched from behind the door.

The cat rubbed up against the caretaker, purring loudly.

The caretaker chuckled. "You like this food, don't you, Puss?" he said, as the cat began to eat. "But you don't like that new cat litter, do you?" he added. He looked at a litter tray on the floor. "That stuff's useless!"

He wandered off, muttering, "And whoever heard of PINK cat litter!"

Jed went over to stroke the cat. He glanced at the cat litter

tray as he passed. Sure enough, it was full of bright-pink pellets. How strange.

Jed looked at the label on the sack next to the tray. This was no ordinary cat litter – it was the missing fuel!

"Meow!" yowled the cat.

Jed gave the cat a hurried pat, and then grabbed a handful of the pellets. He made a trail with the pellets from the boiler room to the manager's office.

He glanced at his watch. The hour was nearly up. "Time to go!" he said, running back to the exhibition.

A few minutes later, Jed's mum appeared. She was smiling.

"That was easier than I thought," she said. "Have you found what you wanted too?"

"Yes thanks, Mum!" Jed replied, smiling back at her.

Jack Be Nimble

Jack be nimble,
And Jack be quick:
And Jack jump over
The candlestick.

The Man in the Wilderness

The man in the wilderness asked me,
How many strawberries grew in the sea?
I answered him as I thought good,
As many red herrings as grew in the wood.

Fire on the Mountain

Rats in the garden – catch 'em Towser!
Cows in the cornfield – run boys run!
Cat's in the cream pot – stop her now, sir!
Fire on the mountain – run boys run!

If All the World Was Apple-pie

If all the world was apple-pie,
And all the sea was ink,
And all the trees were bread and cheese,
What should we have for drink?

This Little Piggy

This little piggy went to market,
This little piggy stayed at home,
This little piggy had roast beef,
This little piggy had none,
And this little piggy cried
Wee-wee-wee-wee-wee!
All the way home.

Bob Robin

Little Bob Robin,
Where do you live?
Up in yonder wood, sir,
On a hazel twig.

Welcome to the Haunted House!

Step in through the rusty gates –
Be quiet as a mouse.
We're going to sneak, and take
A peek, inside the Haunted House!

Upstairs in the dusty bedrooms
Skeletons are getting dressed.
Vampires brush their hair and teeth.
All the spooks must look their best!

An empty suit of shiny armour
Is clanking loudly down the hall,
To a party in the ballroom –
It's the Spooks' Secret Ball!

So while the party's in full swing,
Be quiet as a mouse.
Tiptoe out while you still can –
Escape the Haunted House!

Five Little Monkeys

Five little monkeys walked along the shore;
One went a-sailing,
Then there were four.
Four little monkeys climbed up a tree;
One of them tumbled down,
Then there were three.
Three little monkeys found a pot of glue;
One got stuck in it,
Then there were two.
Two little monkeys found a currant bun;
One ran away with it,
Then there was one.
One little monkey cried all afternoon,
So they put him in an aeroplane
And sent him to the moon.

Baby Bear

Brett was a baby bear cub who just couldn't wait to grow up into a big bear.

"I wish I was big and strong like Daddy," he told Mummy Bear one morning. "Then I could leave home and look after myself, just like a grown-up bear."

Mummy Bear smiled and ruffled Brett's furry little head.

"Don't be in such a hurry to grow up," she whispered. "You're my beautiful baby, and I love taking care of you."

"I'm not a baby," cried Brett. "I'm a big bear!"

And to show Mummy just how big he was, he leapt into the river and splashed around until, after a bit of a fight, he managed to catch a tiny, wriggling fish in his mouth.

"See," he cried triumphantly, proudly showing Mummy Bear what he had caught. "I can catch fish like a big grown-up bear."

"Well done," cried Mummy. Then she dipped a large paw into a pool and flipped out a huge fish.

"Oooh," gulped Little Bear. "I guess I've still got a bit to learn about fishing."

Mummy and Brett sat down beside the river and began to gnaw on their fish.

Suddenly, a large eagle began circling above them. He had a huge, curved beak, and razor-sharp claws.

Brett leapt to his feet and began waving his paws around wildly.

"Go away, you big brute!" he bellowed at the top of his voice. The eagle ignored him and prepared to dive.

Mummy Bear lifted up her head and gave a gentle growl. The eagle took one look at her sharp teeth and long claws and soared back up into the sky

"Oooh," gulped Little Bear. "I guess I've got a bit to learn about scaring eagles."

Mummy Bear smiled kindly. Then she picked up Brett and gave him a big, hairy hug.

"There's plenty of time to grow up. You should enjoy being my baby bear first."

"Yes," agreed Brett, snuggling up to his Mummy's warm, soft fur.

"Being your baby is kind of nice, after all!"

I Love You, Daddy

"You're getting tall, Little Bear," said Daddy Bear. "Big enough to come climbing with me."

Little Bear's eyes opened wide in surprise.

"Do you really mean that?" said Little Bear.

Daddy Bear nodded. He led Little Bear to a giant tree.

Little Bear tried to scramble up onto the lowest branch. He tumbled backwards.

Daddy Bear tugged Little Bear.

"You can do it!" he whispered.

And suddenly, Little Bear found that he could.

"I love Daddy," thought Little Bear.

"You're getting brave, Little Bear," said Daddy Bear. "Daring enough to gather honey."

Little Bear gasped. "Could I really?"

Daddy Bear winked. He led Little Bear to another tree and pointed to a hole in the trunk. Little Bear reached out his paw. A furious buzzing filled his ears. Little Bear pulled his paw back.

"Just be quick," Daddy Bear said. "You have thick fur. The bees can't hurt you. You can do it!" he smiled.

And suddenly, Little Bear found that he could.

"I love Daddy," thought Little Bear.

"You're getting smart, Little Bear. Smart enough to find a good winter den," said Daddy.

Little Bear grinned. "Do you really think so?"

"I know so," said Daddy Bear.

Little Bear set off. "Not too far from food," said Daddy Bear. "Ready for when spring comes."

Little Bear sniffed the wind.

"Look for high ground," said Daddy Bear, "to keep us dry." "Somewhere safe and warm and away from danger."

"Here!" called Little Bear as he disappeared into a deep cave.

Daddy Bear followed. He looked all around. "Perfect! Well done, Little Bear!"

"I love Daddy," thought Little Bear.

"Did I climb well?" Little Bear asked on the way home.

"You did!" replied Daddy Bear.

"Was I brave?" asked Little Bear.

"You were!" answered Daddy Bear.

"Did I find a good den?" asked Little Bear.

"The very best!" smiled Daddy Bear.

Suddenly, Little Bear felt very tired, but there was something he wanted to say.

"I love you, D..." began Little Bear. But he didn't finish.

Daddy Bear gently lifted Little Bear onto his back and began the long journey home. "I love you, too," he whispered.

Ride a Cock-horse

Ride a cock-horse to Banbury Cross,
To see a fine lady upon a white horse;
Rings on her fingers and bells on her toes,
And she shall have music wherever she goes.

Miss Jane Had a Bag

Miss Jane had a bag and a mouse was in it;
She opened the bag – he was out in a minute.
The cat saw him jump and ran under the table,
And the dog said, "Catch him, kitty, soon as you're able."

My Little Cow

I had a little cow, hey diddle, ho diddle!
I had a little cow, and I drove it to the stall;
Hey diddle, ho diddle! And there's my song all.

Round About

Round about, round about,
Runs the little hare,
First it runs that way,
Then it runs up there.

Pop Goes the Weasel

Half a pound of tuppenny rice,
Half a pound of treacle.
That's the way the money goes,
Pop! goes the weasel.

Old Mother Goose

Old Mother Goose,
When she wanted to wander,
Would ride through the air
On a very fine gander.

The Shopping Trip

"I wish I could buy a new bike," said Eddie, gazing into the bike shop window. "Mine's useless."

"Me too," said Josh. "But neither of us has any money."

They both sighed.

Eddie grabbed Josh's arm. "I know!" he said. "We could make our own money, running errands!"

"Try Mrs Cole next door," said Eddie's mum, when they told her their plan. "She might have a few jobs you could do."

Mrs Cole gave Eddie and Josh a huge shopping list. "Make sure you don't forget anything!" she snapped. Mrs Cole was always bad-tempered.

Eddie and Josh spent ages at the supermarket finding everything on the list. They paid at the checkout and stared at the pile of heavy bags.

"How are we going to carry all this?" Josh asked.

"Wait here!" Eddie told Josh. And he raced off.

Eddie returned with his baby sister's pram and Rusty, his dog.

"Put the shopping in the pram, Josh," he said, tying Rusty's lead to the pram. "Rusty can pull the shopping home for us."

But as Josh put the last bag in the pram, Rusty spotted a cat and darted after it.

"Quick!" yelled Eddie. "Follow that pram!"

As Rusty and the pram passed Mrs Cole's house, Rusty dodged a lamp post and *Crash!* The pram smashed right into it.

Five big shopping bags flew through the air and then landed with a terrible clatter.

Mrs Cole rushed out. "Tidy up this mess!" she shouted. "And then buy me some more shopping with your own money!" She marched back into her house and slammed the door.

Then a window opened. It was Mr Cole. "That chase was the funniest thing!" he said, laughing. "Come over here."

The boys went over to the window. "Don't tell Mrs Cole I paid you," he whispered, handing them the money. "And don't worry about the cost of the shopping, either. Seeing something so funny was worth it!"

He smiled. "But I think I'll go shopping myself – in the car!"

Tent Trouble

Ross and Jane were on the swings in the campsite playground.

"This is great!" said Ross, pushing off as hard as he could.

Sam and Kim, who were staying in the tent next door to Ross and Jane, were watching Ross and Jane play.

"Swings are for babies," said Sam.

"It's fun," said Jane.

"We're going to have better fun," said Sam.

"What are you going to do?" asked Ross.

"We're not telling you," said Kim. And they ran off.

"I wonder what they're going to do?" said Jane.

"Let's follow them," said Ross.

Ross and Jane followed Sam and Kim across the campsite back to where their tents were pitched.

From behind the bushes, they watched Sam and Kim pulling out all the tent pegs in their parents' tent one by one

and laughing.

"Now this is fun!" Sam was saying to Kim.

"The tent is going to fall down!" said Jane to Ross.

"Look out!" shouted Ross, as loudly as he could.

Sam's mum and dad

looked out of the tent... just as it fell down around their ears with a huge flapping noise!

"Ouch!" cried Sam and Kim's dad, as a pole hit him on the head.

Sam and Kim's parents crawled out of the ruined tent.

"I wonder what happened?" said Sam and Kim's dad. "We must have not put it up properly."

Sam and Kim were trying hard not to giggle.

Ross stepped out from behind the bushes.

"It wasn't the wind," he said. "Sam and Kim pulled out all the tent pegs."

"They did," agreed Jane.

"Sam! Kim!" shouted their parents.

"It was a joke!" said Sam.

"I have a better joke," said their mum. She picked up the tent pegs and gave them to Sam and Kim.

"Put the tent back up!" she said.

The White Feather

Duck was waddling around the farmyard when she saw a large white feather floating in the pond. She fished it out with her beak, and put it in her tail.

But when Pig saw Duck, he burst out laughing. "You look so silly!" he cried, rolling round in the mud.

"I thought I looked pretty," said Duck, feeling a bit sad.

Duck went to find Horse. "Do I look silly with my nice new feather?" she asked him.

"I think you look wonderful!" said Horse, kindly. "But that feather isn't yours. It belongs to Chicken."

"Then I'll give it back at once," said Duck. She went straight to see Chicken. "I've got your feather," said Duck. "I'm so sorry."

"Thank you!" cried Chicken, putting the feather back in her own tail, where it looked just perfect.

"And how beautiful you look with your fine yellow feathers, Duck," she said.

Duck waddled out into the farmyard feeling very pretty indeed!

Lost Bananas

One day, Elephant was stomping through the jungle when she found a huge bunch of bananas lying under a tree. "Someone must have lost these," she thought. "I'll go and ask Snake."

Elephant found Snake sunbathing on a rock. "Have you lost these bananas, Snake?" asked Elephant.

"How delicioussssss! But they're not my bananassss!" hissed Snake, and slithered into the trees.

"I'll just leave them here, then," said Elephant. "Someone will find them." And she plodded back into the jungle.

A giraffe with a long, thin neck came swaying past, and spotted the bananas sitting on the rock.

"What a pity! Someone has lost their dinner," she said, bending down to eat the thick jungle grass.

"Someone must want those bananas!" said Parrot, watching from a tree.

Suddenly she heard a rustling in the branches…

… and lots of monkeys came swinging through the trees!

"Of course! Monkeys love eating bananas!" cried Parrot.

"Wow, what a fantastic bunch of bananas!" said the monkeys. "Let's have a *huge* jungle feast! Come on everybody! Let's eat!"

Tumbling

In jumping and tumbling we spend the whole day,
Till night by arriving has finished our play.
What then? One and all, there's no more to be said,
As we tumbled all day, so we tumble to bed.

Lie a-Bed

Lie a-bed,
Sleepy head,
Shut up eyes, bo-peep;
Till day-break
Never wake:–
Baby, sleep.

There Was a Crooked Man

There was a crooked man, and he went a crooked mile,
He found a crooked sixpence against a crooked stile;
He bought a crooked cat, which caught a crooked mouse,
And they all lived together in a little crooked house.

Three Wise Men of Gotham

Three wise men of Gotham
Went to sea in a bowl:
And if the bowl had been stronger,
My song would have been longer.

I Hear Thunder

I hear thunder, I hear thunder,
Hark! don't you? Hark! don't you?
Pitter, patter raindrops, pitter, patter raindrops,
I'm wet through, I'm wet through.

Mr East's Feast

Mr East gave a feast;
Mr North laid the cloth;
Mr West did his best;
Mr South burnt his mouth
With eating a hot potato.

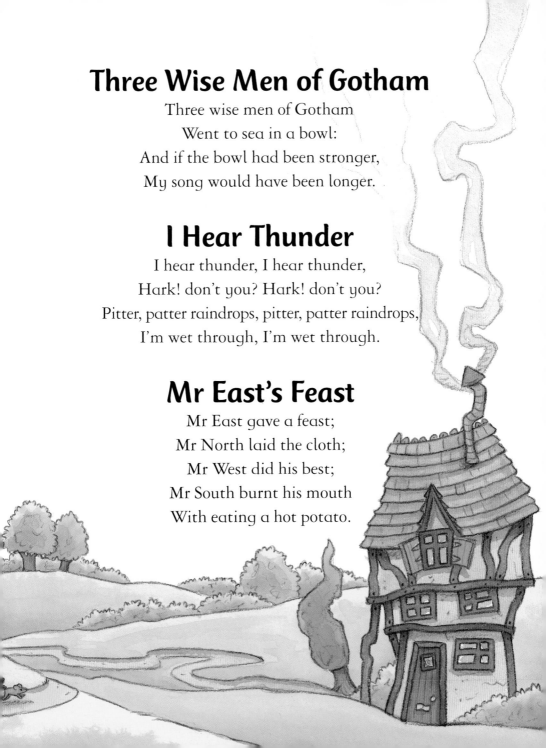

Cooking Up a Storm

I've got my biggest cauldron
Heating up upon the fire,
And I've gathered the ingredients
This fine spell will require!

A handful of cat's whiskers,
The tails from three young pups,
A big ladle full of eyeballs,
And froggy slime – two cups!

Bangs and crashes shake the windows,
It's raining cats and dogs,
Outside the storm is stirring up
A nasty shower of frogs!

For, although it may be August,
So sunny, bright and warm,
You'd better run for cover –
I've cooked up the perfect storm!

When Dreams Come True

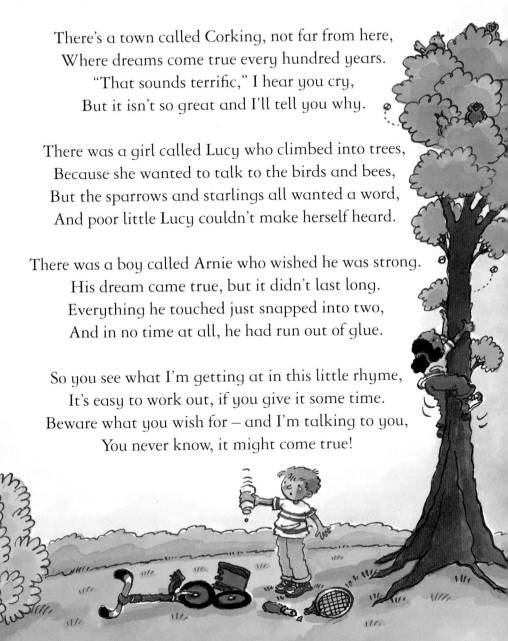

There's a town called Corking, not far from here,
Where dreams come true every hundred years.
"That sounds terrific," I hear you cry,
But it isn't so great and I'll tell you why.

There was a girl called Lucy who climbed into trees,
Because she wanted to talk to the birds and bees,
But the sparrows and starlings all wanted a word,
And poor little Lucy couldn't make herself heard.

There was a boy called Arnie who wished he was strong.
His dream came true, but it didn't last long.
Everything he touched just snapped into two,
And in no time at all, he had run out of glue.

So you see what I'm getting at in this little rhyme,
It's easy to work out, if you give it some time.
Beware what you wish for – and I'm talking to you,
You never know, it might come true!

A Big Box of Hats

Billy was looking for his roller skates. He looked under his bed. He didn't find his roller skates but he did find a big box. There were some hats inside that Billy had never seen before.

One of them was a space helmet.

"Brilliant!" said Billy. He loved spacemen. Pulling out the helmet, he put it on.

Whoosh! All of a sudden, Billy was a spaceman on the Moon. He could see the stars. He was standing by his very own spaceship.

"They must be magic hats!" he thought. "Wow!"

An alien came jumping by. It could jump very high because it was on the moon. "Floop!" it said.

"Hello!" said Billy. The alien jumped up and up.

"That looks like fun," said Billy.

"Floop!" said the alien, jumping again.

Billy jumped too. He could jump so high! Six times higher than he could on the Earth.

Then Billy heard a very loud and anxious "Floop!" from the alien.

The alien had jumped higher still – but this time it hadn't come back down again. It was spinning out of control, away from the Moon!

Billy jumped as high as he could. He just managed to grab hold of the alien's arm and pull it back down again.

"Floop!" said the alien gratefully.

"Be more careful next time," said Billy. He went back into his spaceship and closed the door ready for blast-off, then took off his helmet.

Whoosh! Suddenly, Billy was back in his bedroom. He looked out of the window at the sky.

A spaceship flew across.

"Goodbye, Floop!" smiled Billy.

Birthday Surprise

It was Patch the sheepdog's birthday on Bluebell Farm.

"Fred, it's your job to decorate the barn for the surprise birthday party," said Jenny. "I'm going to bake the cake."

"No problem!" said Farmer Fred.

Farmer Fred sent Patch up to the top field to count sheep, then he and the animals began to decorate the barn. They piled all the presents on a bale of hay and hung up a big banner. Then Farmer Fred started blowing up balloons. He puffed and puffed. It was taking *ages*!

"Never fear, I've an idea!" he cried, and disappeared into his workshop. Not long after the door swung open and out stepped Farmer Fred pushing a strange-looking machine.

"This," he said proudly, "is the Puffomatic Balloon-blower. All I need to do is flick this switch and we'll have those balloons blown up before you can say *Party Poppers*!"

Farmer Fred pulled some balloons over the neck of the machine and flicked a switch. Within seconds the balloons had reached their full size.

"There," said Farmer Fred.

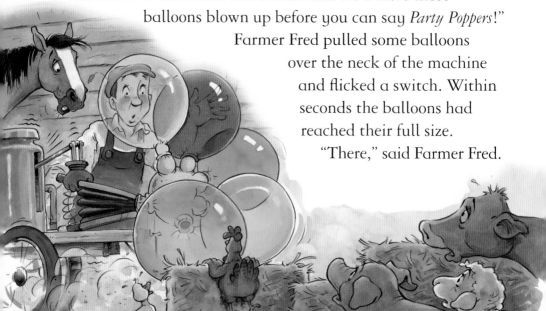

But the Balloon-blower didn't stop. The balloons grew bigger and bigger until suddenly…

BANG! They burst. Bales of hay flew this way and that. All the animals ran out of the barn as fast as they could.

Patch raced down from the field. "Woof! Woof!" he barked. "What's going on?"

Patch couldn't see Farmer Fred anywhere. He went into the barn. There were bits of machine and bales of hay all over the place. But Farmer Fred was nowhere to be seen.

"Woof! Woof!" barked Patch, as he spotted Farmer Fred's hat sticking out from beneath a bale of hay. Patch pushed the bale of hay out of the way. And there was Farmer Fred.

"Woof! Woof!" barked Patch, licking Farmer Fred's face.

"Thanks," laughed Farmer Fred. "I think that perhaps the Puffomatic…err… thingy could do with a bit more work."

Just then, Jenny came into the barn with a bone-shaped cake.

"Ah, you're all here," she smiled, looking around. "And I can see that you've been busy decorating. Now we can start the surprise birthday party."

"Happy Birthday, Patch!" shouted everyone.

The Powerful Spell

The sky went black and the villagers ran for their lives. "Help! Help!" they cried, as they dashed for the safety of the castle. "The dragon is back!"

Hovering above the thick stone castle walls, its giant, red, scaly wings outstretched, was a huge and terrible dragon.

"Curses!" snarled the dragon, blasting the castle with fire. "Just missed a tasty bite to eat."

The village had been a target for the dragon almost every day since it had taken up residence in the nearby mountains. Fortunately, help was at hand – from a very unlikely source.

Alberta the absent-minded witch happened to zoom over the mountains on her broomstick, just as the dragon was returning to its nest. Alberta, who always travelled too fast and who never looked where she was going, sailed right into the dragon's open mouth.

Now, to find yourself stuck in the foul-smelling mouth of a dragon would be enough to send even the nicest witch off the deep end. "Newts and toads!" she snapped, thinking the dragon had had the cheek to try to eat her. "You've bitten off a bit more than you can chew this time!"

Raising her magic wand, she cast a brilliant spell: *'A fearsome dragon you will not be. I'll wave this wand, just wait and see!'*

Then she conjured herself back to the comfort of her own home for a cup of slime tea.

Blissfully ignorant of the fact that a powerful spell had been cast upon it, the dragon returned to its nest.

"Dragon ahoy!" shouted the look-out the next day, as the dragon swooped down on the village once more. But the dreaded fiery jets of dragon breath never came, for when the enchanted dragon drew a deep breath and blew out with all its might, millions of sweet-smelling flower petals fluttered downwards from its gaping jaws.

Inside the castle, everyone started to laugh.

The dragon knew it was making a ridiculous spectacle of itself. No dragon worth its salt would blast a castle with flower petals! It flew away and never came back.

"Good riddance to you," the king called after the dragon.

Then everyone enjoyed a wonderful celebratory feast, before they lived happily ever after.

Joey's Favourite Colour

One starry night Joey the polar bear cub, and his friends were admiring the night sky. It was so colourful that even Joey and his friends were bathed in soft colours.

"Wow, it's beautiful!" gasped Joey.

"I've never seen such a purple sky," exclaimed Hare.

"Purple's my favourite colour," said Fox.

"And it's mine too," decided Hare. "What's your favourite colour, Joey?"

Joey scratched his head and frowned.

"I don't really know," he said finally. "I've never really thought about it before."

That night, while Joey was asleep, he had a wonderful dream

about a rainbow. The rainbow was full of the brightest colours you could imagine. They were so lovely that Joey just couldn't decide which one he liked best.

The next morning, Joey told his mum about his dream.

"I just don't know which colour I like best," he told his mum. "How can I decide?"

Mummy Polar Bear laughed. "You don't have to have a favourite colour," she said kindly. "I like lots of colours because they make me feel happy."

Joey looked around thoughtfully. He wondered what colours made him feel happy. He loved all the bright colours of the rainbow. But he couldn't decide which colour made him feel the happiest.

That evening, as Joey snuggled up beside his mum he felt happy and safe. And all of a sudden he

knew what his favourite colour was. It was the colour of the snowy world he lived in. It was the colour of his two best friends. And, best of all, it was the colour of his lovely mum. Joey's favourite colour was white! How could it be anything else?

To Market, to Market

To market, to market, to buy a fat pig,
Home again, home again, dancing a jig;
Ride to the market to buy a fat hog,
Home again, home again, jiggety-jog.

To Market, to Market

To market, to market, to buy a plum bun;
Home again, home again, market is done.

Two Little Men

Two little men in a flying saucer
Flew round the world one day.
They looked left and right,
And they didn't like the sight,
So then they flew away!

Higgledy Piggledy

Higgledy piggledy,
Here we lie,
Picked and plucked,
And put in a pie!

Jack, Jack, the Bread's a-Burning

Jack, Jack, the bread's a-burning,
All to a cinder;
If you don't come and fetch it out
We'll throw it through the window.

My Rabbit

I love my rabbit,
Who's soft and furry,
And wiggles his nose
All the time – it's his habit.

245

All the Pretty Horses

Hush-a-bye, don't you cry,
Go to sleep, little baby.
And when you wake,
You shall have
All the pretty little horses.
Blacks and bays,
Dapple greys,
Coach and six white horses.
Hush-a-bye, don't you cry,
Go to sleep, little baby.

Five Little Owls

Five little owls in the old elm tree,
Fluffy and puffy as owls should be,
Blinking and winking with big round eyes
At the big round moon that hung in the skies.
As I passed by I heard one say,
"There'll be mouse for supper, there will today."
Then all of them hooted, "Tu-whit, tu-whoo!
Yes, mouse for supper, hoo hoo, hoo hoo."

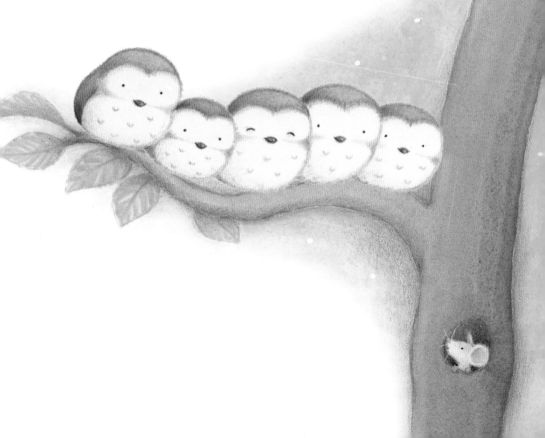

The Mice and the Douglas Fir Cones

Long ago, a family of mice lived in a forest. It was a wonderful place to live, with plenty of nuts and berries to eat, but there was one problem. A fox also lived in the forest, and he was always trying to catch them for his supper.

Finally the mice came up with a plan. One of them would keep watch, while the other mice gathered food. That way, if the fox came along, the mouse on guard would give a squeak of alarm and the family could race back to their home beneath the Douglas fir tree.

The plan worked well, until one day the youngest mouse took his turn as lookout. He soon got bored keeping watch for the fox, and after a while he began chatting to a frog who was hopping around under the tree.

Soon the conversation turned to the forest and the animals that lived there, until at last the fox's name was mentioned.

"I am very pleased that you and your family live here now," croaked the frog.

"I used to have a lot of trouble with that sly old fox – but he much prefers eating mice to frogs, so he doesn't bother me any more."

Suddenly the little mouse remembered that he was supposed to be watching out for the fox. He took a quick look around and, to his horror, he spotted the sly creature hiding beneath the branches of the Douglas fir tree. Worse still, the fox had his beady eye on the mouse's unsuspecting family, who were busy gathering food. He was ready to pounce!

"Run! It's the fox!" squeaked the little mouse at the top of his voice – but it was too late. The mice scampered around frantically, searching for somewhere to hide.

All at once, the father mouse saw that the ground around the tree was covered with Douglas fir cones.

"Hide in the cones!" he squeaked, squeezing in between the fir cone's scales as far as he could.

The fox was very confused. One moment the ground was covered with fleeing mice – the next moment they had all disappeared! He didn't think of looking at the fir cones scattered around. But we know what happened, don't we? And to this very day, if you look at a Douglas fir cone you can still see the hind legs and the tails of the mice sticking out.

The Birds, the Beasts and the Bat

Once upon a time, the birds and the beasts had an argument and decided to fight one another. All the birds from miles around gathered together in the trees as they waited for the battle to begin.

"Whose side are you on?" the birds called to the bat, who was hanging by his feet from one of the branches.

"Yours, of course," replied the bat. "As you can see, I have wings, just like you."

Meanwhile, on the ground, the beasts were gathering. "Whose side are you on?" they shouted up to the bat.

"Yours, of course," the bat replied. "As you can see, I have fur and teeth, just like you."

The fierce battle began, and at first the birds were winning. Owls and eagles swooped down on mice and rabbits, and the bat was right behind them.

"I'm glad I am on your side," the bat told the birds.

Then the tables turned. Wolves, foxes and cats joined forces

to attack the birds, and as soon as he saw that the beasts were winning, the bat was right behind them.

"I'm glad I am on your side," the bat told the beasts.

Every time there was a break in the fighting, the bat flew back and forth between the birds and the beasts. One minute he was up in the trees, making up stories about what the beasts were planning, the next he was underground in the beasts' den, telling tales about the birds.

After some time, the birds and the beasts began to think that the battle might not be such a good idea after all.

A golden eagle made the first move. He flew down and spoke to a wolf, who was the leader of the beasts.

"The world is big enough for all of us," said the eagle. "There is no reason why we shouldn't all live happily, side by side."

"Let us live in peace," agreed the wolf.

The birds and the beasts were pleased that the fighting was over and began to celebrate. But as they talked about the battle, they realised that the bat had changed sides many times and had spread stories about everyone. Angrily, they turned on the bat, who quickly flew away. And ever since, the bat has hidden away in dark towers and deserted buildings during daylight, only daring to come out at night.

Aesop's moral: Someone who tries to trick others has no friends.

The Lost Valley

Deep in the steamy jungle there was a secret valley that had lain undisturbed since life on Earth began.

A few local people knew about the valley, but they kept well away. You see, stories had been told that terrifying beasts prowled through the lush forests. And it was true – something terrifying did lurk in that valley. For in it lived the last Diplodocus dinosaurs in the world.

One day, a circus owner called Terrible Tony heard about the valley, while tracking down magnificent wild animals for his travelling circus.

"With any luck," he thought, his eyes glinting wickedly, "the monster will be some kind of dangerous animal that will earn me lots of money!" He was determined to find the valley.

Tony armed himself with stun guns, giant nets and even a lasso. He stocked up with provisions and set sail down the river in an inflatable raft.

The further Tony travelled into the jungle, the wilder it became.

One morning, the ground began to shudder. The trees parted and a giant creature burst out of the jungle. It was as long as a town square.

If Tony had had any sense, he would have run for his life. Instead he yelled, "Over here!"

The Diplodocus couldn't hear him. Tony's shouts sounded like tiny, faraway squeaks. However, it had spotted the bright orange raft and made straight for it.

Tony fired a round of darts from his stun gun at the huge creature and waited for it to keel over.

The Diplodocus just shook itself lazily and looked a little bit annoyed. It studied the tiny red-faced man that was irritating it, then bent down and seized Tony in its mouth.

But the Diplodocus, being a plant-eater, didn't eat Tony. Instead, it tossed him away. Then it picked up the raft and hurled it after him.

Tony flew out of the valley and over the hills beyond.

Luckily for him, he landed safely, with an almighty splash, in a distant lagoon.

A few moments later, his raft hit the water right beside him. Tony paddled across that lagoon to the town on its banks as fast as he could go. Then he hailed a taxi to the airport, boarded a plane and never, ever went back to the valley.

Meeting the Diplodocus changed Tony forever. He shut down his circus and released all the animals safely back into the wild.

And the herd of Diplodocus lived happily ever after.

Treasure Map

Pirate captain Jenny and her band of
ruthless pirates were very excited. They
were on the hunt for treasure!

Captain Jenny showed them all the
treasure map. There was an 'X' marked on
it. It was six steps from a rock.

"There'll be gold doubloons and silver
sovereigns, rubies red as blood, sapphires
bluer than the sky and diamonds worth
more than this entire ship!" she said.

Billy the cabin boy was as excited as everyone else. "I'd
really like a gold doubloon," he thought. "Just one." But he
didn't think that he'd be allowed any of the treasure. He was
too young.

The pirates landed on the beach. "Come on, me hearties!"

cried Jenny, jumping off the
ship into the shallows with a big
splash.

On the beach there was a big
rock, just as the treasure map
had promised.

Captain Jenny took six steps
to the left. "One, two, three,
four, five, six."

"Here we go!" she cried.

"Hooray!" cheered the pirates. They started to dig a hole with their shovels in the hot sun. Soon everyone was sweating. They dug and dug and dug – but there was no treasure.

"Oh dear," said Captain Jenny.

"No treasure!" said Bosun Bob.

"Maybe it's a fake map," said Crewman Charlie.

They were all fed up. Then Billy looked at the map again.

"Er, Captain," he said.

"What, Billy?" said Captain Jenny.

"I think the map might be upside down," said Billy.

Captain Jenny looked at the map again. "Do you know, Billy, I think you might be right!" she said.

Captain Jenny took six steps to the right. "One, two, three, four, five, six."

The pirates dug a new hole.

"Treasure!" they all cried.

"Thanks to Billy," said Captain Jenny. "And as a reward, Billy, you can have a dozen gold doubloons!"

Poor Old Robinson Crusoe!

Poor old Robinson Crusoe!
Poor old Robinson Crusoe!
They made him a coat of an old nanny goat,
I wonder how they could do so!
With a ring a ting tang,
And a ring a ting tang,
Poor old Robinson Crusoe!

Jack Sprat

Jack Sprat could eat no fat,
His wife could eat no lean,
And so between the two of them
They licked the platter clean.

Rub-a-Dub Dub

Rub-a-dub dub, three men in a tub,
And who do you think they be?
The butcher, the baker, the candle-stick maker,
Turn them out knaves all three.

Solomon Grundy

Solomon Grundy,
Born on Monday,
Christened on Tuesday,
Married on Wednesday,
Sick on Thursday,
Worse on Friday,
Died on Saturday,
Buried on Sunday,
That was the end
Of Solomon Grundy.

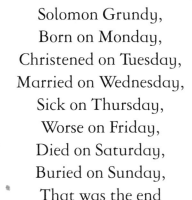

Me, Myself and I

Me, myself and I –
We went to the kitchen and ate a pie.
Then my mother she came in
And chased us out with a rolling pin.

Swan Swam Over the Sea

Swan swam over the sea –
Swim, swan, swim,
Swan swam back again,
Well swum swan.

Tiger Footprints

It was a very hot day in the jungle. Tiggy and Mac were playing near the waterfall.

"Wheee!" shouted Tiggy, as she slid on the wet rocks.

Mac was watching a funny-looking frog. It croaked loudly and then hopped away.

"Where are you going?" asked Mac.

When the little frog didn't answer, Mac ran after it.

"Wait for me!" cried Tiggy.

The twins chased the frog through the leafy jungle.

"Look!" shouted Mac suddenly.

Tiggy tumbled to a stop behind him. In front of them sat a whole family of funny-looking frogs.

"The little frog was hopping back home," said Mac.

Tiggy was tired after their long chase. "I want to go home," she groaned.

Mac looked around. They had never been here before. He didn't know how to get home.

"I wish Mum were here," sighed Mac. "She always knows the way home."

As the two cubs looked around, Tiggy noticed a trail of footprints on the soft jungle floor. The footprints were round

– and very big.

"Maybe they'll lead us home," said Mac.

The little tigers followed them carefully, and at the end, they came across a baby elephant.

"This isn't home," said Tiggy. And the two cubs ran away as fast as their little legs could carry them. Finally, the little tigers had run far enough and they stopped for a rest.

"Look! We've made a trail, too," said Mac.

The pair looked back at the footprints that followed them.

"Let's make some more," cried Tiggy. And they ran faster and faster, making a zigzagging trail of tiger footprints.

Then Tiggy noticed some more footprints nearby.

"Those look just like ours," she said, "but much bigger."

"Mum!" they both shouted together.

And the little cubs began to follow the big tiger footprints back through the leafy jungle to where...

... Mum stood waiting.

"Come on, you two little tigers," she said, smiling at her cubs. "Time to go home!"

Two Heads Are Worse Than One

Clay and Rye were fed up with their parents always giving them chores to do – so, one evening, they decided to run away.

The boys hadn't gone far when they realized that they'd accidentally wandered into Monster Forest. And not only were they lost, but there was something large and heavy coming towards them.

The boys shrank back in fright. A huge monster appeared, green and warty, like a giant toad. It had two heads. One looked kind and friendly, but the other looked bad-tempered.

"Oh, hello," said the friendly head when it saw them. "Company at last. It's very nice to see you…"

"That's enough small talk," growled the ugly head. "I'm going to eat them."

Rye buried his head in his brother's coat.

"We can't eat them, Bad Head. They're far too skinny. Nothing but skin and bone." And the nice head winked at the two boys, as if to say, "Don't worry. I'll look after you."

"Um," agreed Bad Head. "We'll keep them prisoners. Fatten them up a bit, and then eat them."

They all spent a busy day in the forest
looking for food, and when evening fell,
they sat beside a warm fire and talked.
Good Head said that having to feed a
few chickens now and again wasn't such
a bad thing if you had a warm house to
live in and a soft bed, and the boys had
to agree that the life they'd run away from
wasn't so bad after all.

"What nonsense," grumbled Bad Head, rather sleepily.

Good Head winked at the boys. Bad Head was lolling
forward, yawning. Soon he was fast asleep and snoring loudly.

"Quickly," whispered Good Head. They hurried as fast and
as quietly as they could out of the forest.

"Thank you," whispered the boys to Good Head.

"My pleasure," said Good Head. "Now hurry."

Clay and Rye scampered across the open fields towards
home as fast as they could.

Then they heard voices behind them.

"They got away!" Bad Head was
shouting. "You useless monster. Why
didn't you stop them?"

The voices faded into the forest
and the boys ran home. And they
never ventured into Monster Forest,
or complained about their chores,
ever again!

Sports Day

It was Sports Day at school. First there was the running race. All the animals lined up.

"On your marks, get set, GO!" said Mrs Beak, the teacher. Jed Giraffe had long legs. He won the running race.

Next was a beanbag race. Lucy Lion kept her head very still. She won the beanbag race.

Then there was a hopping race. Mikey Monkey won the hopping race.

But poor Helga Hippo didn't win a single race.

That playtime Helga sat on her own, feeling sorry for herself. "I'm no good at anything," she thought.

Then she heard loud shouts from the pond. Mikey had slipped in!

"Help!" he called. "I can't swim!"

"I can't swim, either!" said Jed.

"I can't swim either!" said Lucy.

"Help!" cried Mikey, desperately.

Helga could swim. She jumped in and saved Mikey. "I might not be a fast runner, a good beanbag balancer or a great hopper," she said. "But I can swim!"

"Well done, Helga!" said Mrs Beak.

A Stormy Day

"Lunch time!"

It was time for the builders to eat. The builders went to their hut to drink tea and eat sandwiches.

Digger had a rest. Dumper had a rest. Dozer had a rest.

Then a storm cloud came over. The wind began to blow and the rain began to fall.

"*Meow*!" mewed the cat who lived on the building site.

"The cat will get wet," said Digger.

"Her kittens will get cold," said Dumper. The cat was afraid. She hid her kittens in Digger's scoop.

"Look!" said the builders, when they came back from their lunch. The cat and her kittens were fast asleep curled up in Digger's scoop.

The builders took the cat and the kittens to the hut to keep them safe and dry from the storm.

Princess Prissy

King Fusspot liked everything to be just so. He had his own Rule Book, covering such vital matters as the number of brush strokes his daughter Princess Prissy's royal hair should receive before bed.

Secretly, Princess Prissy thought that her father's Rule Book was just silly, but she never dared to say anything.

Now the Stinky Bog Monster had never read the Rule Book. So when he crashed through Princess Prissy's window one dark night, he didn't give a second thought to the broken glass and slimy trail he was leaving behind him, as he carried the princess off kicking and screaming.

"My poor daughter!" wailed King Fusspot the next morning. "Stuck in that stinking, disorganized lair!"

This was too good a chance to miss for Prince Smarmy. He swiftly struck a deal with the king, ensuring the princess's hand in marriage in return for her safe rescue.

Now, Prince Smarmy knew King Fusspot's Rule Book well, and knew all the proper procedures to follow when rescuing princesses. One very important rule was that a prince had to appear on a gleaming white charger. It was when he was hiding behind a tree outside the Bog Monster's lair, cleaning the mud off his horse before riding to the rescue, that the prince caught sight of Princess Prissy.

Her clothes were torn and covered in stains, and her hair was a filthy mess. The prince's heart was torn with anguish. His darling princess – what had that beastly Bog Monster done to her?

Just then, as he prepared to leap onto his charger to rescue her, the Bog Monster himself appeared.

"Hello there, Boggy darling!" cried Princess Prissy. And with that, she planted a kiss on his cheek! The prince cried out in horror.

"Not you!" cried the princess, catching sight of Prince Smarmy. "If you've come to rescue me, get lost! I'm not coming home – ever! At last I've escaped all those silly rules. All that niceness, and prettiness, and good manners. I'm free! I like being rude and horrible. I've got my darling Stinky Bog Monster to thank for it, and you're too late – we got married last night!"

There was nothing else for it. Prince Smarmy had to admit defeat and head home.

On the way, he noticed a muddy puddle in front of him.

"Why not?" he thought, and rode his horse straight through it, splattering both of them with mud. He laughed out loud. "You never know," he thought. "Perhaps the princess was right, after all. Some rules are just silly."

And he rode through every single puddle all the way home.

A Jittery Journey

The moon's like a wizard's face up in the sky,
The night is as black as a cat.
The trees' branches rustle and wave as you pass,
Then reach down to snatch off your hat.

The wind wants to whisper a secret to you,
An owl hoots, "Noo! Noo! Mustn't tell!"
You can hear a dog howling (or is it a wolf?)
And the chimes of a distant church bell.

A monster is lying in wait by the path –
With hundreds of feet and big teeth!
Or is it a tree fallen, struck in a storm,
With toadstools growing beneath?

Quick! Is that a light you can see through the wood?
Hurry up, there are bats flying round!
Here you are at the gate – Mum opens the door,
And you're home once again – safe and sound!

It's Raining

It's raining cats and dogs,
And warty toads and frogs,
And red-kneed bats and bowler hats.
It's raining big fat hogs.

It's raining needles and pins,
And rusty cans and tins,
And things I don't like – such as bits of bike.
It's raining wheelie bins.

It's raining apples and pears,
And dolls and teddy bears,
And silly pigs in curly wigs.
It's raining plastic chairs.

It's raining bacon and eggs,
And washing lines and pegs,
And cowboy suits and exotic fruits.
It's raining hairy legs.

It's raining ducks and drakes,
And chocolate bars and cakes,
And glasses of milk and colourful silk.
It's raining garden rakes.

Farmyard Chase

Mother Hen sat on her nest and shook out her soft, fluffy feathers. She had an egg to keep warm. She had been sitting there for hours.

"I'm hungry," thought Mother Hen.

Suddenly, Mother Hen saw a patch of sunlight by the barn door. She had an idea. She rolled her egg carefully over into the sun and packed some hay round it. "That will keep you warm," she said to her egg. "I won't be long."

And off she went to find some corn.

Horse came trotting up to the barn. He was hungry, too. He saw the hay by the barn door.

"Yummy!" he neighed, as he pushed his smooth, velvety muzzle into the hay. Bump! Horse's nose nudged Mother Hen's egg.

The egg rocked, and then it rolled. It rolled across the yard.

"Oh no!" neighed Horse. He trotted after the egg as it tumbled towards a pile of apples under the apple tree.

Pig was snuffling around the apple tree as the egg rolled past his nose.

"Oh no!" squealed Pig. "Catch that egg before it cracks!" And he scampered after the egg as it tumbled into the grassy meadow.

Sheep was munching the tufty grass in the meadow as the egg rolled past her.

"Oh no!" bleated Sheep. "Catch that egg before it cracks!" And she skipped after the egg as it tumbled down the hill.

At the bottom of the hill, Cow was lying down, having a rest after lunch. Bump! The egg bounced against Cow's nose.

"Ouch!" mooed Cow. "What was that?" And she stared at the egg. Horse, Pig and Sheep came running down the hill.

"Catch that egg before it cracks!" they called.

"I have caught it," replied Cow.

"My egg!" clucked Hen, flapping her way down the hill.

Just then, there was a loud *Crack!*

"Someone must have cracked it!" clucked Hen. *Crack!* The crack got bigger still.

Suddenly, the egg cracked wide open. Out hopped a soft, fluffy ball of yellow feathers.

"It was me!" cheeped the little fluffy chick. "I cracked it all by myself!"

Jungle Hide-and-Seek

One day Little Elephant was walking through the jungle.
He hadn't gone far when he bumped into Giraffe.

"Hello," called Little Elephant. "Do you want to play?"

Giraffe peered down at Little Elephant and smiled.

"Okay," he said. "You can play hide-and-seek with me, Zebra
and Crocodile. Close your eyes and count to one hundred, then
come and find us."

So Little Elephant closed his eyes and counted to one hundred,
which took a very long time because he was only a very little
elephant. Finally, he opened his eyes and began to search the
jungle for his friends.

He searched through the long grass but he didn't see Zebra
hiding among the tall blades. He searched among the acacia
trees but he didn't see Giraffe hiding between the tree trunks.

He searched the watering
hole but he didn't see
Crocodile hiding in the
shallows. He searched and
searched but he couldn't
find any of his friends.
By midday, Elephant
was feeling so sad that he
decided to call it a day.

"I give up," he shouted.
"You are all too good at

hiding for me."

Then he lay down among some rocks to rest.

One by one, Giraffe, Zebra and Crocodile crept out of their hiding places and went in search of Little Elephant. But they couldn't find him anywhere.

They made so much noise stomping around that Little Elephant woke up and groaned.

"Hey, that rock just groaned," gasped Giraffe.

"I'm not a rock," said Little Elephant. "It's me, Little Elephant."

"So it is!" cried Zebra.

"That's amazing," smiled Crocodile. "Your grey skin makes it hard to see you when you are hiding among the rocks. Just like my green skin helps me to hide in watering hole."

"And my stripes help me hide in the long grass," said Zebra.

"And my patches help me hide among the tall trees," said Giraffe.

"Hooray," cried Little Elephant happily. "I'm good at hiding – just like you!"

The Wolf and the Crane

Once upon a time a greedy wolf was gobbling up an enormous meal when he got a bone caught in his throat. The wolf tried coughing… then he tried swallowing… then he tried drinking, but the bone would not move up or down. It was well and truly stuck, and he couldn't eat a thing. As the days passed, the wolf got thinner and thinner.

One morning, the wolf noticed a crane flying overhead and he had an idea.

"You have such a wonderful long bill," he said to her, when she had landed. "You could do me **a great service** and save my life. I have a bone caught in my throat, so I cannot eat, and I am starving. With your long beak, you could reach down into my throat and pull the bone out for me."

The crane felt very nervous about putting her head into a hungry wolf's mouth After all, he could be planning to eat her.

"I'd like to help," the crane replied, "but I'm afraid that you might bite my head off."

"Why would I do that?" the wolf replied innocently. "In fact, I'd be so grateful to you that I would give you a reward."

The crane was tempted by the thought of a reward, so she agreed to do as the wolf asked.

The wolf opened his mouth, and the crane reached down into his throat with her long bill. She was relieved to find that the wolf was telling the truth and that he really did have a bone stuck there. So she grabbed it with her beak and pulled it out.

As soon as the crane had pulled out the bone, the wolf turned around and began to walk away.

"Just a minute! What about my reward?" called the crane.

"I've given you your reward already," the wolf replied. "I let you take your head out of my mouth without biting it off, even though I am starving. You should be very grateful for that!"

Aesop's moral: Never expect a reward for helping the wicked.

Little Mouse

I have seen you, little mouse,
Running all about the house,
Through the hole your little eye
In the darkness, peeping sly,
Hoping soon some crumbs to steal,
To make quite a hearty meal.
Look before you venture out,
See if kitty is about.
If she's gone, you'll quickly run
To the pantry for some fun;
Round about the dishes creep,
Taking into each a peep,
To choose the daintiest that's there,
Eating crumbs without a care.

Sing a Song of Sixpence

Sing a song of sixpence,
A pocket full of rye.
Four and twenty blackbirds,
Baked in a pie.

When the pie was opened,
The birds began to sing;
Wasn't that a dainty dish,
To set before the king?
The king was in his counting house,
Counting out his money;
The queen was in the parlour,
Eating bread and honey.
The maid was in the garden,
Hanging out the clothes;
When down came a blackbird
And pecked off her nose!

The Ungrateful Tiger

Once there was a village that was plagued by tigers, so that the children couldn't play outside and the people were afraid to leave their homes. At last the villagers had had enough, and they dug a deep pit to trap the beasts.

One day, a man was on his way to visit the village when he heard a growl coming from below the ground. The man walked toward the noise and found a tiger stuck in the pit.

"What are you doing down there?" the man asked the tiger.

"I'm stuck," the tiger replied. "I was walking along minding my own business when I fell into this hole, and now I can't get out again. I'm so hungry and thirsty! Please help me."

"But if I help you to get out, you might eat me," the man replied. "After all, you did say you were hungry."

"I wouldn't do that because I would be so grateful," the tiger assured him.

The man hated to see animals suffering, so he got a tree branch and used it to help pull the tiger out of the hole.

When the tiger was safely out of the hole the man continued on his way.

Suddenly, he felt the tiger's hot breath on his neck.

"What are you doing?" cried the man.

"I am going to eat you!" the tiger replied.

"But that's not f-f-fair," the man stammered. "You said you would be grateful!"

"I am," the tiger replied. "But humans dug that trap, and you are a human, so I am going to eat you."

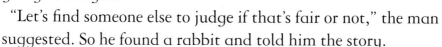

"Let's find someone else to judge if that's fair or not," the man suggested. So he found a rabbit and told him the story.

"I think you had better show me what happened," said the rabbit. So they all went back to the hole in the ground.

"Show the rabbit exactly where you were," the man told the tiger. So the tiger jumped into the pit once again.

"Repeat what you said," said the man. And the tiger did.

The rabbit listened carefully. "In my opinion, it is not fair for you to eat this man," he said, when the tiger had finished. "He did not dig the hole! You should be grateful for his help."

"All right," agreed the tiger. "I promise not to eat him. Now will you help me out of this hole?"

But the rabbit and the man shook their heads, for how could they know if the tiger was telling the truth?

Mowgli and Baloo's Lessons

One day Bagheera, the black panther, was watching Baloo, the big brown bear, teach Mowgli the Law of the Jungle. There was so much to learn that Mowgli started getting things wrong and Baloo cuffed him softly around the ears. Mowgli was so cross that he hid in the trees.

"He's so small," said the black panther. "How can you expect him to learn so much?"

"A man cub is a man cub, and must learn all the Law of the Jungle," replied Baloo. "Nothing is too small to be killed. That's why I hit him, but softly."

"Softly, indeed, old Iron Fist," snorted Bagheera.

"Better he gets the odd pat from me than come to harm through ignorance," replied Baloo.

"At the moment I'm teaching the **Master Words of the Jungle** to protect him from all the jungle creatures. I'll call him and he will say them. Come, Little Brother."

Mowgli slid down a tree trunk.

"My head is ringing," the boy complained, looking annoyed.

"I come for Bagheera, not you, Baloo!"

Baloo was a little upset by this because he loved Mowgli.

"Man cub, why don't you tell Bagheera the 'Master Words of the Jungle,' said Baloo.

"Master Words for which people?" said Mowgli, who was delighted to show off. "The jungle has many tongues."

Then he rattled through the Words of the Animals, the Birds and the Snakes. When he had finished he clapped his hands and made horrible faces at Baloo.

"One day I'll lead my own tri? through the branches. We'll t? branches and dirt a? old Bal? sang Mowgli.

"Mowgli," growled Baloo. ? ? been talking with the Monke? ?ople. They're evil."

Mowgli looked at Bagheera to see if the panther was angry, too, and Bagheera's face looked like cold ice.

"When you hurt my head, they came down and gave me nuts and said I should be their leader. No one else cared," he sniffed.

"They have no leader! They lie," said Bagheera.

"Well, I like them. They play all day," pouted Mowgli.

"Listen," said the bear, and his voice rumbled like thunder. "They have no Law. They creep around and spy. They boast and chatter and pretend to be great when they are not. We of the jungle ignore them even if they throw dirt at our heads."

As he spoke, a shower of nuts and twigs rained down.

The evil Monkey People shrieked above. One of them had had a brilliant idea. He'd decided that Mowgli would be a useful person to have in their tribe. He could teach them how to make huts like the ones humans lived in. With Mowgli's help, they would become the wisest people in the jungle.

The Monkey People waited until Baloo, Bagheera and Mowgli were asleep, then they grabbed the little boy and swung him through the treetops.

Mowgli felt sick and giddy as they bounded, crashed and whooped from one tree to the next. He knew that he had to get word back to his friends, for at the speed they were going Baloo and Bagheera would never be able to keep up. Mowgli saw Chil, the kite bird, circling above and remembered Baloo's lessons.

"We be of one blood, you and I. Tell Baloo and Bagheera that Mowgli passed this way."

Meanwhile, Baloo and Bagheera, who had heard Mowgli's cries, followed below. Before long, they came across Kaa, the python.

"What are you hunting?" hissed the snake.

"Monkey People, who have snatched Mowgli," explained Baloo.

"I'll help you hunt them," hissed Kaa.

Just then, there was a shout from above. It was Chil, the kite.

"The Monkey People have taken him to their ruined city."

"Come," said Bagheera. "We must go there at once."
And off they all raced.

Meanwhile, the monkeys had gathered around Mowgli, chattering about how wonderful they were. Mowgli began to think that they were all mad. He was wondering how he could escape when Bagheera raced down the hill and began knocking monkeys left and right. But there were too many, and soon the brave panther was fighting for his life.

"Roll to the water tank," cried Mowgli. "They won't follow."

With a burst of strength, Bagheera threw off his attackers and lunged into the water tank. Just at that moment, Baloo lumbered in and took up the fight. Then Kaa pounced, eager and ready to kill.

Kaa was everything the monkeys feared. With one hiss, the monkeys scattered with cries of "It is Kaa, run, run!"

Mowgli was free from the Monkey People's clutches.

And after that day, he always tried his best to remember everything Baloo taught him.

Monster Munch

I may be big and hairy
And I may look mean and tough,
But I'm a nice, kind monster,
And I've simply had enough!

It's really most distressing
When you scream and run away –
I have no plans to eat you,
All I want to do is play!

Oh, can't you see I'm lonely?
Can't you tell I'm feeling blue?
I've got no friends to talk to,
But I like the look of you!

I'm just about to make some lunch,
And I'd love it if you'd come.
You will? Oh, great, that's perfect!
Ha, ha – I tricked you! Yum!

London Bridge

London Bridge is falling down,
Falling down, falling down.
London Bridge is falling down,
My fair lady.

Build it up with iron bars,
Iron bars, iron bars,
Build it up with iron bars,
My fair lady.

Iron bars will bend and break,
Bend and break, bend and break,
Iron bars will bend and break,
My fair lady.

Build it up with stone so strong,
Stone so strong, stone so strong,
Huzza! 'twill last for ages long,
My fair lady.

Washing Up

When I was a little boy
I washed my mummy's dishes;
I put my finger in one eye,
And pulled out golden fishes.

What's the News?

"What's the news of the day,
Good neighbour, I pray?"
"They say the balloon
Is gone up to the moon."

The Queen of Hearts

The Queen of Hearts, she made some tarts,
All on a summer's day;
The Knave of Hearts, he stole the tarts,
And took them clean away.
The King of Hearts called for the tarts,
And beat the Knave full sore;
The Knave of Hearts brought back the tarts,
And vowed he'd steal no more.

King Arthur

When famed King Arthur ruled this land
He was a goodly king:
He took three pecks of barley meal
To make a bag pudding.
A rare pudding the king did make,
And stuffed it well with plums;
And in it put such lumps of fat,
As big as my two thumbs.
The king and queen did eat thereof,
And noblemen beside,
And what they could not eat that night
The queen next morning fried.

Cobbler, Cobbler

Cobbler, cobbler, mend my shoe,
Get it done by half past two;
Stitch it up, and stitch it down,
Then I'll give you half a crown.

Rain

Rain before seven,
Fine by eleven.

The Clumsy Hippo

Grace the Hippo was having a lovely time wallowing in the waters of Lake Haha, when the flamingos came wading by. They looked so beautiful that Grace rolled onto her back to get a better look.

"**Tut, tut!**" they squawked as Grace showered them with cold water.

"Sorry," said Grace, hanging her head. She was so embarrassed that she heaved herself out of the water and waddled away. "I wish I could move gracefully like the flamingos," she thought. "I'm just so clumsy. I can't imagine why Mum and Dad called me Grace!"

Grace walked sadly along the riverbank. She didn't see Crocodile lounging in the sun until it was too late.

"**Ouch!**" cried Crocodile, as Grace trod on his tail. "Watch where you stomp those great big feet."

"Sorry," said Grace, blushing.

Grace went to eat some grass. She tore up a great hunk and began to chomp on it noisily. She chewed the grass round and round, licked her enormous teeth, and burped!

"**Really!**" said Zebra, who was grazing nearby. "Didn't your parents teach you any manners?'

"Sorry," said Grace. "It just popped out!"

Grace decided to go for a run. She might be a little on the round side, but she enjoyed running. She was having a great time until Meerkat stuck his head out of a burrow.

"Hey, clumsy!" he bellowed. "Do you mind? Your footsteps are shaking my home."

"I beg your pardon," said Grace.

Grace plonked herself beneath her favourite Acacia tree to think. She didn't notice that Anteater was already sitting there until she heard a yell.

"Ouch!" he shrieked. "Get your big bottom off my head."

"Oops! Sorry," said Grace. "I'm so clumsy, I think I'd better keep out of everyone's way today."

She waded sadly back into Lake Haha, dived beneath the surface, and paddled along. Soon she was gliding swiftly through the water. The fish waved happily to her. Then Turtle came and joined her in a game of chase. Suddenly Grace smiled. Now she remembered why Mum and Dad had called her Grace. When she was swimming, she wasn't clumsy at all. In fact, she was really rather 'graceful'.

Little Penguin and Friends

Little Penguin had no one
to play with.

"Why don't you build
a snow den?" suggested
Mummy Penguin.

So Little Penguin used his
tiny wings to scoop up as
much snow as he could into
a pile. It was hard work on his own,

but he kept on until he had made a giant fluffy, white mound
of snow.

He was very tired by now, though, and he was just about to
give up when Little Polar Bear came wandering by.

"What are you doing?" Little Polar Bear asked his friend,
curiously.

"I'm trying to build a snow den," replied Little Penguin. "But
my flippers are very small, and I'm getting very tired."

"Can I help?" asked Little Polar Bear. "My paws
are good for digging in the snow."

So Little Polar Bear began to dig with his big furry paws, and
Little Penguin helped. It was hard work, but they kept on

until they had made a big
snowy cave.

Little Seal came by.

"That looks like fun,"
he said. "Do you need
any help? My fins and
tail are perfect for
patting down snow."

So Little Seal patted
the snow den to make it smooth and shiny, while Little
Penguin and Polar Bear helped. It was hard work, but they
kept on patting until the den gleamed.

Little Fox Pup scampered over to admire their work.

"Shall I use my tail to sweep away the snow?" he offered.
And he swished his tail back and forth to clear a path.

At last Little Penguin's snow
den was finished.

"What shall we do now?"
asked his new friends.

"Play in the snow den,
of course!" laughed
Little Penguin excitedly.
**"It's just the
right size for
four friends!"**

A Tortoise

A tortoise is a funny thing,
And very lazy, too.
To eat and sleep the livelong day
Is all it cares to do.
And when I tried to make it race,
It wasn't any fun.
It tucked its head inside its shell
And simply wouldn't run.

Mr Mole

Oh, Mr Mole, come out of your hole,
And look at the sky so blue.
It must be dark deep under the ground,
And ever so lonely, too.
Oh, Mr Mole, come out of your hole,
Come out in the fresh clean air.
There's snails and bugs and bees that buzz...
and butterflies everywhere.
Oh, Mr Mole, come out of your hole,
And meet the world in the sun.
There's games to play and things to see.
Come out and have some fun!

Squirrel's Nut Pile

One morning, Squirrel scurried around the forest floor. He scampered up trees and then down again. His bushy tail swayed from side to side as he went. He was busy gathering nuts for the winter. When he had collected a big pile, he stopped and scratched his furry ears.

"Now I just need to find somewhere safe to store them," he muttered, looking around. "Somewhere warm and dry and not too far away. And somewhere where the pesky weasels won't find them."

As he peered around hopefully, Rabbit popped up from a hole in the ground. She twitched her nose and smiled at Squirrel.

"Aha," thought Squirrel. "That looks like the perfect place."

"Hello, Rabbit," he called. "Can I store my nuts in your burrow?"

Rabbit shook her head sadly. "Sorry," she replied. "But there won't be enough room for all my babies and all your nuts.

I've just moved out of my old burrow in the beech tree because it was too small for us all."

Squirrel sighed and looked very disappointed. Rabbit felt so sorry for him that she wondered what she could do to help. There must be somewhere Squirrel could keep his nuts. She thought and thought until she had a brilliant idea.

"I know," she cried, thumping her foot with excitement. "Why don't you use my old burrow in the beech tree. It's warm, dry and surely big enough for all your nuts."

"Oh, thank you," cried Squirrel. "That will be perfect. The weasels will never think of looking there, and it's only a hop and skip from my nest,"

After kissing Rabbit on her fluffy cheek, Squirrel scampered away and began storing his nuts in their new hide-away. But he didn't hide every single one of them. He made sure there was a nice big pile for kind Rabbit and her family. After all, one good turn deserves another.

Tiger Tales

Louis and Lisa Lion were just learning to pounce. One day, as they pounced through the jungle, Louis suddenly saw a flash of orange and black in some bushes.

"A striped snake!" Louis whispered. He crouched down and waited for just the right moment, and then he…
"Owwwwow!" came a voice from the bush. "What's got my tail?"

The 'snake' turned out to be attached to a striped little cub.

"Who are you?" asked Louis and Lisa.

"I'm Timmy Tiger," said the little cub. "My mum and dad and I have just moved here from The Other Side of the Jungle."

"We're Louis and Lisa Lion," said Lisa. "Would you like to see what this side of the jungle looks like?"

Timmy said he would love to.

"That's our river," said Louis proudly. "It's really muddy, and fun to paddle in."

"It's very nice," said Timmy, "but it's kind of small. On The Other Side of the Jungle, there's a river that's as wide as fifty tall palm trees laid end to end, and I

once swam across it!"

A little farther along, Louis and Lisa saw Howard Hippo wallowing merrily in the mud. "Hi, Howard!" they called.

"You know," said Timmy, "on The Other Side of the Jungle there's a hippo whose mouth is so big that I can sit inside it!"

"Wow!" said Lisa.

"And," Timmy continued, "my dad's twice as big as an elephant, and he can carry six gorillas on his back! And..."

Timmy stopped in his tracks. In front of him stood two tigers, smiling. They were his mum and dad.

"Mum and Dad, these are my new friends, Louis and Lisa."

"We're delighted to meet you," said Mr and Mrs Tiger.

"And as you can see," Mr Tiger added, "we are very ordinary and normal tigers."

"Timmy told us some amazing things about The Other Side of the Jungle," said Louis.

Timmy looked embarrassed.

Mrs Tiger turned to Louis and Lisa. "Timmy didn't have any friends to play with on The Other Side of the Jungle, so he spent all his time imagining amazing adventures."

"But now that he's got friends like you two to play with," said Mr Tiger, "perhaps he'll have some real adventures, like the ones in his stories!"

Jed's First Day

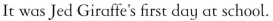

It was Jed Giraffe's first day at school.

"I am too small to go to school, Mum," he said on the way there.

"You're not too small, Jed," said Mum. "Everyone goes to school when they are your age."

"Hello, Jed," said Mrs Beak, the teacher, when they arrived at school.

"I am too small to go to school, Mrs Beak," said Jed.

"Why don't you just go inside and have a look?" said Mrs Beak. "There are lots of other animals here."

But when Jed tried to go into the school he walked into the door. Bump!

"You are certainly not too small, Jed!" said Mrs Beak. "You are too tall! We will have to have school outside," she said.

All the other animals came outside.

"This is Jed," said Mrs Beak.

"Hello, Jed!" they said.

"Hello," said Jed. They looked very friendly.

"We're glad you are here, Jed," said the animals. "School is much more fun outside."

Broken Down

The building site was busy. Digger was busy. Dumper was busy. But Dozer wasn't budging a single centimetre.

Digger scooped up a big pile of sand. "Come and help, Dozer!" he said.

Dumper tipped out a huge pile of bricks. "Come and help, Dozer!" he said.

But Dozer didn't help. Dozer didn't move even a single centimetre.

Dumper and Digger were getting annoyed. They had lots of work to do and they needed Dozer's help.

"Have you broken down, Dozer?" asked Dumper.

Digger stopped scooping sand. Dumper stopped tipping bricks. It was very quiet on the building site. Then there was a loud "*Miaow…*"

"It's a cat!" said Dozer, proudly.

"*Mew! Mew! Mew!*"

"And her kittens!" said Dozer.

The cat and her kittens were in Dozer's scoop. That was why Dozer wasn't moving. He wasn't being lazy and he hadn't broken down.

"The kittens are safe," smiled Dozer.

The Lemur Dance

Louis the Lemur had a secret. He loved to dance, but none of the other lemurs knew, because Louis was very shy. He never went down to the river to play. He never joined in games of hide-and-seek. And when all the other lemurs decided to do a Lemur Dance, Louis would run away and hide.

One day, when the other lemurs were playing in the forest, Louis crept out from his hiding place and began to sway. He closed his eyes and began to twirl. He hummed, and then leaped into the air and spun around and around. He was having such a wonderful time that he didn't hear the other lemurs coming back. When he opened his eyes and saw them, he stopped dancing at once!

"Don't stop!" cried Melanie the Lemur, grabbing his paw. **"You're a great dancer!"**

"Wow," thought Louis, as they twirled around and around. "Dancing with other lemurs isn't at all scary. It's even better than dancing alone!"

After that, Louis always played and danced with the other lemurs. And he was never ever shy ever again.

SSSSHHH!

One morning Lion was very tired, so he curled up for a nap.
He was just dozing off when Monkey began to screech.

"**Ssssh!**" roared Lion angrily. "Can't a lion get any peace?"
Monkey crept away.

Lion settled back down and closed his eyes. He was just
beginning to snore when Elephant came stomping by.

"**Ssssh!**" roared Lion angrily. "Can't a lion get any peace?"

"Sorry," whispered Elephant, and he tiptoed away.

Suddenly there was a loud hiss. It was Snake passing by.

"**Ssssh!**" roared Lion angrily. "Can't a lion get any peace?"

"S...s...sorry," hissed Snake.

Lion closed his eyes again, but it was no use. No matter how
hard he tried, he was much too angry by now to fall asleep.

"What you need is a jungle lullaby," squeaked a little mouse.
"Listen to the whispering breeze, and the stream bubbling
down to the waterhole. Listen to the crickets singing in the
grass. That's a jungle lullaby! Can you hear it?"

But Lion never said a word. He was fast asleep. **Ssssh!**

Stinky the Skunk

Stinky was a little skunk who didn't like her name.
It made her feel ridiculous and often blush with shame.
It didn't even suit her, because she didn't smell…
She always washed her paws and fur, and her tail as well.
"I wish my name was Dancer, Rose or even Fleur…
Or maybe Stripy would be nice, to match my stripy fur."
Her mother smiled kindly. "From now I'll call you Rose."
But as these words were spoken she wrinkled up her nose.
Rose was so excited… she'd lifted up her tail,
And sprayed a stinky, skunky scent – all along the trail.
Rose giggled loudly and said, "I must admit,
When I am excited I do stink just a bit!"

Milly the Kangaroo

Milly was a kangaroo who loved to bounce and hop.
Every time she started – she didn't want to stop!
She bounced around all morning, and every afternoon.
She bounced around the forest, beside the blue lagoon.
"Look at me," she'd chuckle, bouncing to the sky.
"I'm a flying kangaroo, I can bounce so high!"
Milly never got fed up of bouncing up and down,
Even when she went to school or shopping in the town.
Her Mum would hop beside her and offer things to eat,
But Milly never stopped at all – not even for a treat.
And when she snuggled down at night
Beneath the moonlight's beams…
She just kept right on hopping by bouncing in her dreams!

The Old Woman and the Fat Hen

An old woman kept a hen that laid one egg every morning without fail. The eggs were large and delicious, and the old woman was able to sell them for a very good price at market.

"If my hen would lay two eggs every day," she said to herself, "I would be able to earn twice as much money!"

The old woman decided that the best way to make the hen lay an extra egg each day was to feed her twice as much. So besides giving the hen a bowl of corn in the morning, the woman gave her one every evening, too.

The hen was very happy and gobbled up all the extra corn.

Each day the old woman went to the henhouse expecting to find two eggs, but there was still only one – even though the hen was getting fatter and fatter. One morning, the woman looked in the nest box and there were no eggs at all. There were none the next day either, nor any day after that. All the extra food had made the hen so fat and contented that she had become lazy and had given up laying eggs altogether!

Aesop's moral: Things don't always work out as planned.

The Mice in Council

Once there was a family of mice. They would have been very happy, if it weren't for the cat who also lived in their house. Every time they crept into the kitchen to pick up a few crumbs, the cat would pounce, and chase them under the floorboards.

"If we don't do something soon, we'll starve," said the oldest mouse. "We must hold a council to decide on a plan."

All the mice got together, but none of them could come up with an idea that they all agreed on. Finally, the youngest mouse had a brainwave. "We can put a bell on the cat's collar, so we can hear him coming," he said.

The mice agreed that it was an excellent plan, and the young mouse felt very **proud** of himself. Then the grandfather mouse stood up. "You are a very smart young fellow to come up with such an idea," he said, "but, tell me this – who is going to be brave enough to put the bell on the cat's collar?"

Aesop's moral: It is sometimes easy to think of a clever plan, but it can be much more difficult to carry it out.

Crocus the Crocodile

Crocus was a friendly crocodile who never, ever ate other animals. The problem was that no one else knew this.

"Hello!" he called to Antelope and Zebra, as he swam along the river. And he smiled his biggest, toothiest grin. But as soon as they saw him, Antelope and Zebra just hid in the bushes.

"How strange," thought Crocus as he waved to Wild Pig and her babies, and gave them his best smile.

"**Eeeeeee!**" squealed the little piglets, darting away.

Crocus began to cry. "No one wants to be my friend."

"You seem all right to me," said Hippo, who was passing by.

"Do I?" asked Crocus. And he gave Hippo his toothiest smile.

"Ahh," said Hippo. "Now I see the problem. They think you want to eat them with your big teeth."

"But I'm a vegetarian," shouted Crocus at the top of his voice. "I don't eat animals!"

His words echoed around the jungle and through the treetops.

"Did you hear that?" the other animals cried. "Crocus is a vegetarian! Let's make friends with him."

And that's exactly what they did. Of course, Crocus was very happy – but he tried his best not to smile about it too much!

Rama Has Toothache

Rama the tiger was usually very friendly, but one morning she awoke with a loud roar – and she didn't stop roaring all day. Whenever anyone passed her cave, she roared. If anyone asked her what was wrong, she roared. Soon everyone in the jungle was creeping around on tiptoe. Everyone was much too afraid to go near her. Everyone, that is, but Bat.

"What is the matter?" he asked.

"Buzz off!" roared Rama.

Bat shook his head. "I'm not going until you tell me."

"I've got a toothache!" growled Rama angrily.

"Then we will have to pull out your bad tooth," replied her friend.

"Oh, no, you don't," roared Rama. And to make sure that no one touched her tooth, she stuck her head out of her cave and roared so loudly that the jungle shook. "If anyone touches me, I'll bite them," she cried. And just to prove it, she bit a nearby tree.

As she bit, Rama felt something in her mouth move. Her sore tooth had come out in the tree trunk!

"Hooray!" cried Rama happily. "My toothache is gone." But no one was happier than her friends!

Bunny in a Hurry

Tick tock! It's eight o'clock!
Can you tell the time?
Wake up, Bunny! Don't be late!
It's time to rise and shine.

Tick tock! It's twelve o'clock!
No time for any stops!
Bunny has a bouncy lunch,
Munching as he hops!

Tick tock! It's three o'clock!
So many things to do,
Like finding everything he needs
To make a carrot stew.

Tick tock! It's six o'clock!
And something smells delicious!
Hurry, Bunny, eat your stew!
You've got to wash the dishes!

Tick tock! It's seven o'clock!
Shhhh! Don't make a peep.
What a busy day it's been.
Now Bunny's fast asleep!

Jungle Hide-and-seek

Crouching in the jungle,
Roaring by a tree,
Looking for his dinner,
Who can you see?

Deep in the jungle,
Hiding up a tree,
Eating a big banana,
Who can it be?

Down beside the river,
Showing lots of teeth,
Waiting still and silent,
Who's underneath?

High up in the branches,
Noisy as can be,
With bright, shiny feathers,
Who's in the tree?

Creeping through the jungle,
Such a king is he,
Fierce, gold and furry,
Who can it be?

Best Friends

Jamie and Paul were best friends. They sat next to each other in class every day. They played together and ate lunch together every day.

One day at break, Jamie pulled Paul's coat and a button flew off.

Paul and Jamie looked for the button all through break, but they couldn't find it anywhere.

Then the bell rang to say that break time was over.

"We *must* find my button," said Paul, "or my mum will be really cross!" So Jamie and Paul kept looking until they found the button.

Miss Bell told them off for being late.

"It's your fault!" Paul said to Jamie.

"It's your fault!" Jamie said to Paul.

The two friends did not talk to each other in class for the rest of the morning. They did not sit together at lunch.

The first lesson after lunch was games.

"Let's see who can change the most quickly!" Miss Bell said.

Jamie and Paul pulled out their PE bags.

"I'm going to beat Paul," Jamie thought to himself. "I'll show him!"

"I'm going to beat Jamie," Paul thought to himself. "That'll serve him right!"

The two boys raced to change into their shorts and T-shirts.

They finished at exactly the same time.

"I'm first!" cried Jamie, raising his hand. His T-shirt suddenly felt very tight under the arms.

"No, I'm first!" shouted Paul. As he raised his hand as well, he suddenly noticed that his T-shirt was almost down to his knees.

"Why are your clothes so small, Jamie?" asked Billy.

"And why are yours so big, Paul?" asked Miss Bell.

Their friends started to laugh.

"You mixed up your PE bags!" said Tilly.

Jamie and Paul laughed as well. They looked at each other.

"Friends again?" said Jamie.

"Friends again!" said Paul.

Bertha the Goat

It was breakfast time, and Bertha the goat was very hungry.

"Maa," she called as the farmer walked into the barnyard with a bucket of food. But he walked right past Bertha and tipped the scraps into Pig's trough.

"Can I try some?" asked Bertha. And she gobbled up Pig's scraps before he could reply. She only stopped when she saw the farmer pouring milk into Cat's bowl.

"Can I try some?" asked Bertha. And she lapped up the milk before Cat could even reply.

By now Bertha was beginning to feel kind of full, but when she saw the farmer putting hay into Horse's manger she rushed over and she started munching before Horse could say a word.

Suddenly Bertha heard a familiar sound. The farmer was pouring nuts into her trough. Bertha groaned. She had eaten so much that her poor belly was full up and she couldn't eat another bite.

"Can we have some?" shouted all the other animals. "Some greedy goat gobbled down all our breakfasts."

Bertha looked shamefaced. "I promise not to be so greedy ever again," she said.

Matty the Koala

"It's time for your nap," called Matty the baby koala's mum.

"But I'm not sleepy," said Matty. "I want to explore."

"Of course you're sleepy," laughed Mrs Koala. "Koalas are always sleepy. We can go exploring later." And she popped Matty into her pouch and curled up in the eucalyptus tree.

But Matty didn't want a nap – he wanted to explore. When he was sure his mum was asleep, he crept quietly out of her pouch, down the tree and scampered off into the forest.

High in the trees, he spotted a colourful parakeet.

"Yeeah!" he cried, chasing after it. Then he heard a funny sound. Ribbet! Matty looked around and saw a huge, warty toad puffing out its chest.
It looked so funny that he giggled.

Suddenly Matty heard a scary sound. Hisssssssssss!

"It's a snake!" cried Matty.

The frightened little koala ran as fast as his legs would carry him back to the eucalyptus tree, and dived into his mum's pouch.

"Ooooooh," yawned Mrs Koala, smiling down at Matty. "Come on, sleepyhead. It's time to explore."
But Matty didn't say a word.
He was fast asleep after his adventures.

Time for Bed

As dusk fell over the jungle, the elephants huddled together
and prepared to sleep. But Tootles the baby elephant wasn't
ready for bed. He stomped around and drew patterns with his
trunk in the dust.

"Come on, Tootles," smiled Mum. "It's time for bed."

Tootles tried to hide a yawn. "Can't we stay up and play?"
he asked. "I don't want to go to sleep."

"Why not?" asked Mum. "You must be tired after such
a long day."

"I don't want to say," said Tootles
shyly. "You'll think I'm silly."

"I could never think you were
silly," said Mum kindly.
"Tell me what's
troubling you."

Tootles looked up
at his Mum and blushed.
"I don't like the dark," he
admitted. "Why
does it have to be
dark at bedtime? It makes me feel afraid."

Mum looked down at Tootles and smiled. "But the dark
is a good thing," she said. "It's like a soft blanket covering the
world, letting everyone know it's time to go to sleep."

"But I might have bad dreams," said Tootles, who was still not convinced.

"No, you won't," said Mum. "The world is full of good dreams, if you know where to find them. Look up at the sky."

So Tootles looked up at the night sky. It was a moonlit night, and the sky was full of twinkling stars.

"Each star is a good dream, just waiting for you," explained Mum. "And just look at how many there are!"

"Wow!" said Tootles. "There must be millions. I can't wait to go to sleep now ... I wonder how many good dreams I will have tonight!"

Tootles began to count the stars, but before he got to ten, he was sound asleep.

Mum smiled down at him and wrapped her trunk around his warm body. **"Sweet dreams!"** she whispered.

Little Poll Parrot

Little Poll Parrot
Sat in the garret,
Eating toast and tea;
A little brown mouse,
Jumped into the house
And stole it away, you see.

B-I-N-G-O!

There was a farmer had a dog,
And Bingo was his name-O.
B-I-N-G-O!
B-I-N-G-O!
B-I-N-G-O!
And Bingo was his name-O!

Diddlety, Diddlety, Dumpty

Diddlety, diddlety, dumpty,
The cat ran up the plum tree;
Half a crown
To fetch her down,
Diddlety, diddlety, dumpty.

A Duck and a Drake

A duck and a drake,
And a nice barley cake,
With a penny to pay the old baker;
Hippety hop, we're off to the shop,
If she won't come, we'll take her.

Thirty White Horses

Thirty white horses upon a red hill.
Now they tramp, now they champ,
Now they stand still.

A Cat Came Fiddling

A cat came fiddling out of a barn,
With a pair of bagpipes under her arm.
She could sing nothing but fiddle dee dee,
The mouse has married the bumble bee.
Pipe, cat! Dance, mouse!
We'll have a wedding at our good house.

Catch Him

Catch him, crow! Carry him, kite!
Take him away till the apples are ripe;
When they are ripe and ready to fall,
Here comes a baby, apples and all.

Wine and Cakes

Wine and cakes for gentlemen,
Hay and corn for horses,
A cup of ale for good old wives,
And kisses for the lasses.

Wee Willie Winkie

Wee Willie Winkie runs through the town,
Upstairs and downstairs in his nightgown,
Peeping through the keyhole, crying through the lock,
"Are the children in their beds? It's past eight o'clock!"

Hurt No Living Thing

Hurt no living thing:
Ladybird, nor butterfly,
Nor moth with dusty wing,
Nor cricket chirping cheerily,
Nor grasshopper so light of leap,
Nor dancing gnat, nor beetle fat,
Nor harmless worms that creep.

Two Little Dogs

Two little dogs
Sat by the fire,
Over a fender of coal dust;
Said one little dog
To the other little dog,
"If you don't talk,
Why, I must."

The Horse and Rider

The prairie blows the grasses
And whips the horse's mane.
They travel, horse and rider,
Through the sea of amber grain.

Gym Giraffe

Jeremy Giraffe loved going out with his dad to gather juicy green leaves for dinner.

"Remember – the tallest trees have the tastiest leaves, and the tiny top leaves are the tenderest!" his dad would say.

One morning Jeremy decided he wanted to gather leaves on his own, but his neck wouldn't stretch high enough. So Jeremy went back home with his neck hanging down in despair.

"Why, Jeremy, whatever is the matter?" asked his mum. When Jeremy told her, she gave his neck a nuzzle.

"You're still growing," she assured him. But Jeremy couldn't wait for his neck to grow. So he headed to the Jungle Gym to do neck lengthening exercises.

Jeremy spent the next few weeks stretching his neck with all sorts of exercises. Finally, he felt ready to reach for the highest leaves.

Next time Jeremy and his dad went out leaf gathering, Jeremy spotted some juicy leaves at the top of a very tall tree.

"I'm getting those," he said.

"They're so high up!" said Dad. But sure enough, after a big, big stretch, Jeremy reached up and ate them up!

Monkey Mayhem

Mickey, Mandy and Maxine Monkey had finished their breakfast of Mango Munch. Now they were rushing off to play.

"Be careful!" called their mum. "And DON'T make too much noise!"

"We won't!" the three mischievous monkeys promised, leaping across to the next tree. The noise echoed through the whole jungle – Mickey, Mandy and Maxine just didn't know how to be quiet!

Mickey landed on a branch. Maxine and Mandy landed beside him. Just then the branch snapped in two and they shrieked, as they went tumbling down, down, down.

The jungle shook as the three monkeys crashed to the ground, then sprang to their feet.

"Yippee!" the monkeys cheered, brushing themselves off.

The three monkeys then scrambled back up to the top of the trees. They screeched and screamed as they swung through the branches back towards home.

All through the jungle, the animals covered their ears. Nobody would ever keep these three noisy monkeys quiet!

Little Ghost Lost

"Come along, Percy," said Mum. "It's time we took you out for your first proper spooking expedition. And what better night for spooking than Halloween!"

"Just follow us and copy what we do," said Dad. "And don't wander off on your own."

The three ghosts floated up the chimney of their home in the Haunted House, and curled out of the top like wisps of smoke.

"I don't like it out here," said Percy, timidly. "It's too dark!"

"Don't be silly," said Mum. "Ghosts aren't afraid of the dark!"

All through the evening the family of ghosts played ghostly pranks, jumping out and spooking folk, and squealing with delight as they ran away, screaming.

"I bet I could spook someone all on my own!" thought Percy.

Creeping up behind two children, he set his face in its most fearsome expression, then tapped them on their shoulders. But, as the children spun around, Percy froze in horror. He was eye to eye with two gruesome monsters!

Percy screeched and fled into the night. He didn't hear the screams behind him, or see the monsters race home, where they tore off their Halloween masks and panted out their story to their mother. Poor Percy had never heard of trick-or-treating!

Percy flitted down the streets, calling

for his mum and dad. Where had he left them?
Finally he sank down in a doorway.

"I want my mum!" he wailed, and
began to cry. Then something poked and
prodded him with a sharp stick.

"What have we here then?" said a
mean little voice.

"Looks like a young ghostie. Let's
pinch him!" said another nasty voice.
The voices belonged to two goblins.

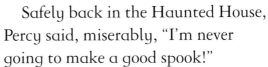

"BOO!" said Percy, pulling a scary face.
"Leave me alone!"

But the goblins just burst out laughing. It takes
a lot to frighten a goblin. "Nothing scares us!" they teased.

"Oh no?" said a deep voice behind them. "How about this!"
The goblins turned to see two huge, terrifying ghosts.

"Aaaaargh!" they cried, fleeing into the night.

"Mum! Dad!" cried Percy in delight. "You found me!"

Safely back in the Haunted House,
Percy said, miserably, "I'm never
going to make a good spook!"

"Yes you will," soothed Mum, tucking
him into bed. "After all, you certainly
scared us! Next time, stick close!"

"I promise," said Percy, and in
no time at all he was sound asleep,
dreaming of ways to spook goblins.

My Goat

My goat will eat most anything;
A pair of socks, some garden string,
A cardboard box, my favourite hat,
A bag of corn, the kitchen mat,
My brand new boots, a rubber ball,
He'll eat anything at all!
And if there's any room, at last...
He'll munch a bunch of fresh green grass.

Bat, Bat

Bat, bat,
Come under my hat,
And I'll give you a slice of bacon;
And when I bake,
I'll give you a cake,
If I am not mistaken.

Hungry Tiger

Hungry tiger in a tree,
Watching you,
Watching me.
You best take care,
My little friend,
Unless you want a sticky end!

Dolphin Song

The day is grey, but the dolphins play,
They dance and leap and sing.
They dive through the waves,
And they're ever so brave!
A dolphin's a wonderful thing.

Yankee Doodle

Yankee Doodle went to town,
Riding on a pony;
He stuck a feather in his cap
And called it macaroni.

Yankee Doodle keep it up,
Yankee Doodle dandy,
Mind the music and the step,
And with the girls be handy.

Snorri Pig

Snorri pig had a curly tail.
A curly tail, a curly tail,
His head was round as the top of a pail,
Hey up for Snorri pig!

Snorri pig had big brown eyes,
Big brown eyes, big brown eyes,
And he was lord of all the sties,
Hey up for Snorri pig!

When Snorri pig met a lady sow,
A lady sow, a lady sow,
He'd smile and bend his knees full low,
Hey up for Snorri pig!
But when he met another boar,
Another boar, another boar,
He'd tread him into the farmyard floor,
Hey up for Snorri pig!

The Fox and the Goat

One hot day, a thirsty fox was searching for something to drink. At last he found a well in a farmyard. He stuck his nose over the edge, but the water was too far down. Very carefully, he balanced on the side, trying to reach the cool, clear water. But though his nose was so close that he could smell it, he still couldn't quite reach the water.

The fox made one last try, stretching out his tongue with all his might. SPLASH! he toppled right in.

The sides of the well were so slippery that when the fox tried to climb out, he just kept sliding back down. He was stuck!

After a while, a goat came by looking for a drink. He was surprised to see the fox in the water.

"What on earth are you doing down there?" he asked.

"Just cooling down," replied the fox. "The water in this well is the best for miles around. Why don't you jump in and try it."

The goat was very hot and thirsty, and the water did look very refreshing, so he jumped in to join the fox.

"You're right!" said the goat, taking a long drink and relaxing in the water. "It's lovely and cool down here."

Soon the goat decided that it was time to go on his way.

"How do we get out?" he asked.

"That is a bit of a problem," the fox admitted. "But I've got an idea. If you stick your legs out, you can wedge yourself in the well. Then I can climb on your back and jump out."

"That's all very well, but what about me?" the goat bleated.

"Once I've climbed out, I can help you get out," the fox explained.

So the goat wedged himself against the walls of the well and the fox clambered onto his back and leaped out.

"Thank you," laughed the fox, as he turned to leave.

"Hold on! What about me? How am I going to get out?" cried the goat.

"You should have thought about that before you jumped in," replied the sly fox – and off he ran.

Aesop's moral: Look before you leap.

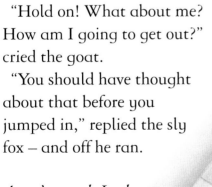

The Town Mouse and the Country Mouse

Once a town mouse went to visit his cousin in the country. The country mouse was very pleased to see his relative and made him as welcome as he could. Although he only had simple food in his pantry, he offered his cousin everything that he had: peas, barley, nuts and cheese.

The town mouse picked at the food, while his country cousin made do with a piece of barley straw.

"I don't know how you can put up with such boring food," the town mouse said after dinner. "Your life here is so dull. It's much more fun in town. We have streets full of carriages and smartly dressed people, and wonderful food for the taking. Why don't you come and see?"

So the country mouse packed a bag and the cousins set off.

It was dark by the time they arrived in town, and the country mouse was dazzled by the bright city lights. At last, the two mice crept into the house where the town mouse lived.

The country mouse stared in wonder at the velvet chairs

and fine furniture. On the dining table lay the remains of a banquet. After offering his cousin a seat, the town mouse ran back and forth bringing delicacies for his cousin to try — lobster, venison with red wine sauce and finally (though the country mouse was so full he could hardly move) strawberry cake and cream. The little mouse had never eaten such a fantastic feast!

Suddenly the door slammed and a bunch of noisy young men with two large dogs burst into the room. The terrified mice fled and hid under a cupboard, shaking with fear as the two dogs growled at them. Finally, when the men had gone to bed and the dogs had settled down to sleep, the country mouse crept out from his hiding place.

"Goodbye, cousin," he whispered. "This fine living is all very nice, but I would rather enjoy a crumb of bread in peace, than feast on this delicious food and live in constant fear."

Aesop's moral: It's better to enjoy bread and water in peace, than fine food in fear.

Vicky the Very Silly Vet

"Good morning!" called Vet Vicky as she opened the door to her surgery. "How are all my animals today?"

She lined up the breakfast bowls and animal feed on the table and began to put out the food. Then... DING! went the doorbell.

"Oh!" cried Vicky. " My first patient is here already!" As quickly as she could, she put the bowls in the cages – but didn't look to see who was getting what! Patch the puppy got the bird seed, Hickory and Dickory the mice got the dog food, Percy the Parrot got the cat food and Tabby got the mice's sunflower seeds! What's more, Vicky had left all the cage doors wide open.

Fortunately, this had happened before and the animals knew just what to do. Hickory and Dickory found their sunflower seeds in Tabby's basket, Tabby discovered her cat food in Percy's cage, Percy pecked at his bird seed in Patch's cage, and Patch found his dog food in the mouse cage.

"Come in," said Vicky to her first patient. Then a thought crossed her mind. Hadn't she left the cage doors open? She gulped. What dreadful mess would there be?

But the clever animals were all back in their own cages. Vicky saw the clean and tidy room and grinned. "Treats for tea!" she whispered.

Barmy Builder Benny

One morning, Benny the builder arrived at Polly the postlady's house.

"I want you to build a Wendy house for my grandchildren," she said. "It should have two doors, five windows, and a sloping roof."

Polly left for the post office, and Benny went out to start work. He tried to remember everything that Polly had said, but he got confused. Was it five windows and two doors? Or two windows and five doors? Was the roof flat or sloping? Benny decided he would just have to do the best he could.

When Polly got home from work what a surprise she had! The Wendy house's roof was flat. There were five doors on one side of the house, and two windows on another side.

"It's all wrong!" said Polly. "How will you fix it in time?"

Benny didn't have a chance to answer, because just then Polly's five grandchildren arrived.

"Look! A Wendy house!" they cried. "There's a door for each of us! And we can climb on the roof! Thank you, Granny!"

"Well, I think you should thank Benny," said Polly, smiling.

Benny smiled too. "I just did my best," he said.

Shoe the Horse

Shoe the horse and shoe the mare,
But let the little colt go bare.

Little Fishes

When I was a little boy,
I washed my mother's dishes.
I put my finger in my ear,
And pulled out little fishes.
My mother called me good boy,
And bid me pull out more.
I put my finger in my ear,
And pulled out four score.

Three Ducks in a Brook

Look, look, look!
Three ducks in a brook.
One is white, and one is brown.
One is swimming upside down.
Look, look, look!
Three ducks in a brook.

There Was a Rat

There was a rat, for want of stairs,
Went down a rope to say his prayers.

A Dog and a Cat

A dog and a cat went out together,
To see some friends just out of town;
Said the cat to the dog,
"What d'ye think of the weather?"
"I think, Ma'am, the rain will come down.
But don't be alarmed, for I've an umbrella
That will shelter us both,"
Said this amiable fella.

The Wise Old Owl

The wise old owl
Sat on a branch,
His big round eyes shut tight.
"Tu whit, tu whoo,"
He softly called.
"Tu whit, tu whoo!
Goodnight!"

The Chipmunk
and the Bear

One day a bear was walking through the woods.

"I am so strong, I can do anything," he shouted out proudly, lifting up tree trunks with one paw to search for food.

"Not anything!" said a small voice.

The bear looked down at the ground and saw a chipmunk with his head sticking out of a hole.

"You can't stop the sun from rising," the chipmunk said.

"I'm sure I could," boasted the bear. "In fact, I will do it tomorrow. Tomorrow the sun will not come up!"

So the bear and the chipmunk sat side by side all night,

facing the east, waiting to see if the sun would rise.

"The sun will not come up," the bear chanted.

"The sun will come up," the chipmunk chanted, but very quietly under his breath.

As morning approached, the sky began to lighten.

"The sun will not come up. I command it!" the bear shouted.

Slowly, the sun began to appear, and the chipmunk started to laugh.

"The sun has made a fool of you!" he taunted.

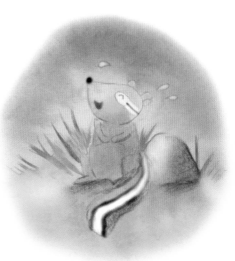

The bear was furious. His paw shot out and pinned the chipmunk to the ground.

"We'll see who the biggest fool is now!" he growled.

The chipmunk realised he had made a big mistake and should not have teased the bear.

"I am sorry," he squeaked. "You are right! I am worthless, and you are one of the greatest and strongest animals in the world. Please just lift your paw so I can catch my breath to tell you how much I admire you."

The bear was very vain, so he raised his paw a little. Quick as a flash, the chipmunk darted away, but as he escaped, the bear's claws scratched his back. And, to this day, the chipmunk still carries the claw marks on his back as a reminder to think twice before making fun of someone.

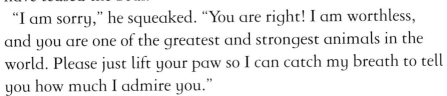

Mousie

Mousie comes a-creeping, creeping.
Mousie comes a-peeping, peeping.
Mousie says, "I'd like to stay,
But I haven't time today."
Mousie pops into his hole,
And says, "Achoo! I've caught a cold!"

In April

In April's sweet month,
When leaves start to spring,
Lambs skip like fairies,
And birds build and sing.

Horsey, Horsey

Horsey, horsey, don't you stop,
Just let your feet go clippety clop,
The tail goes swish and the wheels go round,
Giddy up, we're homeward bound!

Six Little Mice

Six little mice sat down to spin,
Kitty passed by and she peeped in.
"What are you doing, my little men?"
"Making coats for gentlemen."
"Shall I come in and cut off your threads?"
"No, no, Mistress Kitty, you'd bite off our heads."
"Oh, no, I'll not; I'll help you to spin."
"That may be so, but you can't come in."
Says Kitty: "You look so wondrous wise,
I like your whiskers and bright black eyes;
Your house is the nicest house I see,
I think there is room for you and for me."
The mice were so pleased that they opened the door,
And Kitty soon had them all caught on the floor.

Slippery Snake

Oh, I wish I was a slippery snake,
Oh, I wish I was a slippery snake,
Oh, I'd slither across the floor
And slip under the door,
Oh, I wish I was a slippery snake.

All Around the Barnyard

All around the barnyard
The animals are fast asleep.
Sleeping cows and horses,
Sleeping pigs and sheep.
Here comes the cocky rooster
To sound his daily alarm.
Cock-a-doodle-doo!
Wake up, sleepy farm!

Jenny Wren

As little Jenny Wren
Was sitting by the shed,
She waggled with her tail,
And nodded with her head.

Frog Went a-Courtin'

Frog went a-courtin' an' he did ride,
A bunch of roses by his side.
He rode up to Miss Mousie's door,
Gave a loud knock and gave a loud call.
He said, "Miss Mousie, are you in?"
"Yes, kind sir, I sit and spin."
He took Miss Mousie on his knee,
And said, "Miss Mousie, will you marry me?"

Sparrow Got Up Early

Sparrow got up early,
At the break of day,
And went to Jenny's window,
To sing a roundelay.
He sang a song of love
To pretty Jenny Wren,
And when he got unto the end,
Then he began again.

Dame Trot and Her Cat

When Dame Trot had her dinner
Kitty would wait,
And was sure to receive
A treat from her plate.

Fearless Fireman Fred

Fred hurried into the fire station with a bag of nice plump sausages. It was his turn to cook lunch for the firemen on the shift.

"Ooops!" he said, as he bumped into Benny the builder, who had come to repair the door.

Suddenly the alarm bell rang.

"Emergency!" cried the firemen, sliding down the pole and into their fire-fighting gear.

"What about the sausages?" cried Fred.

"I'll look after them for you!" called Benny.

The emergency was in Tony's Pizza Parlour – one of the pizza ovens had caught fire!

"We'll have that blaze out in a jiffy," said Fred.

"Thank you!" said Tony, as the firemen took their equipment back to the truck. "I can get back to baking pizzas now!"

"Look!" said Fred. "Smoke up ahead!"

NEE-NAW! went the siren as the engine raced to the scene of the fire. The smoke was coming from the fire station!

"Sorry, fellows," said Benny, running out. "I burnt the sausages."

Fortunately, Fred had an idea. "Don't worry, guys," he said. "A yummy extra-large pizza will be a perfect lunch for all of us!"

Potty Polly Postlady

"Good morning, Polly!" said Mr Price the postmaster. "Your postbag is all ready – and it looks extra-full today!"

Polly tore around the corner of Jackson Road on her bicycle. But her bike started to get slower and slower. She realized she had a puncture.

"Oh no!" said Polly. "I'll have to walk my round today!"

Polly rushed and hurried, but by eleven o'clock her postbag was still half full. Then suddenly she saw something that gave her a brilliant idea.

"Jack, may I borrow your skateboard, please?" Polly asked.

Polly had never been on a skateboard before. She wibbled and wobbled… then WHOOSHED down the street.

Polly finished her round at lightning speed. "This is quicker than walking," she said, "and much more fun than my bike!"

At five to twelve Polly staggered through the door of the post office. "I'm back, Mr Price," she gasped.

"Well done, Polly!" said Mr Price. "Benny the builder brought back your bike. We'll have to mend that puncture right away."

"Oh, there's no hurry, Mr Price," said Polly. "I've found a much better form of transport for a potty postlady like me!"

The Farm Show

Farmer Jones was very excited. It was the day of the Sunnybridge Farm Show.

Mrs Jones was entering the Jam-making Competition, and Farmer Jones was entering almost everything else.

"Perhaps you should just enter one thing," said Mrs Jones.

"But there are so many prizes to win," laughed Farmer Jones. "How could I possibly choose? Right, Max?"

Max, Farmer Jones' sheepdog, wagged his tail. He was looking forward to the Farm Show too.

"Pansy is sure to win the Prettiest Pig," said Farmer Jones, as he and Max made their way to the pig sty where Pansy lived.

But Pansy had been rolling in something very dirty and very smelly.

"Phwah!" gasped Farmer Jones.

"Woof!" barked Max, running back to the farmhouse to fetch some of Mrs Jones' extra-strong laundry soap. Farmer Jones used the soap to make a bath.

But it was no good. Pansy was just too dirty and too smelly. They would never get her clean in time.

"Double bother! It doesn't look like I'll be winning the prize for the Prettiest Pig this year," said Farmer Jones. "But Bonnie is sure to win the prize for the Whitest Lamb."

Farmer Jones borrowed some of Mrs Jones' best shampoo and made a bath for Bonnie.

"In you go!" he said, plonking Bonnie into the tub. Farmer Jones began to scrub away. He closed his eyes and began to sing:

"Oh, what a beautiful morning!
Oh, what a beautiful day!
I have a wonderful feeling
I'll win some prizes today!"

"Woof!" barked Max. He tugged at Farmer Jones' sleeve.

"What is it?" asked Farmer Jones.

But it was too late. Bonnie was bright pink.

Farmer Jones had picked up Mrs Jones' hair dye instead of shampoo!

"Bother!" said Farmer Jones. "It doesn't look like I'll be winning the prize for the Whitest Lamb this year. But Chloe is sure to win the prize for the Smartest Cow."

Max fetched Chloe from the meadow. Farmer Jones tied her up and found a brush.

"We'll soon have you gleaming," said Farmer Jones. But Chloe had other ideas. As soon as the brush touched her side, she began to wriggle and squirm.

Farmer Jones had forgotten that Chloe was ticklish! Chloe would not stand still. She would never be ready in time.

"Botheration!" said Farmer Jones. "Now what am I going to do?"

"Are you ready?" shouted Mrs Jones from the farmhouse. "I don't want to be late for the Jam-making Competition."

"Double botheration!" said Farmer Jones. "I've run out of time. It doesn't look like I'll be entering any of the competitions this year."

Later, at Sunnybridge Farm Show, Mrs Jones won first prize in the Jam-making Competition.

Farmer Jones watched as other farmers won the rest

of the competitions, one by one.

"Oh, if only I could enter just one little competition," said Farmer Jones.

"Woof!" barked Max. He ran around in circles pretending to round up some invisible animals.

Suddenly, Farmer Jones understood. "Of course! The Sheepdog Competition," he said.

A few minutes later, they were in the ring. Farmer Jones whistled and Max herded the sheep this way and that. The sheep were herded into the pen in record time.

"And the winners are Farmer Jones and Max," said a voice over the loud speaker. The crowd clapped and cheered.

Later, Farmer Jones showed Mrs Jones the shiny cup they had won.

"It's like I always say," said Farmer Jones happily. "It's best to concentrate on just one thing."

Mrs Jones peered over the cup she had won for her jam.

"Yes, dear," she said, winking at Max.

Fancy Flying

Penelope Parrot and her mum, Portia, were having a wonderful afternoon watching the Fancy Flying Display Team. Penelope could hardly believe her eyes, as she saw the birds swoop and speed through the sky, doing their amazing tricks and wonderful stunts.

"I want to be just like them," thought Penelope.

Penelope had only learned to fly a short time ago – so she didn't really know how fast or how far she could go.

"I think you need some expert training if you want to be a Fancy Flyer," said Mum.

"But I don't know any experts," said Penelope.

"I know an expert," said Mum. "My uncle Percy has just arrived for a visit. He was a member of the original Fancy Flying team!"

So Percy and Penelope practised and practised, but Penelope couldn't stop spinning and crashing and falling.

"Well, Penelope, are you ready to be a Fancy Flyer?" Mum asked, when she got home.

"Oh yes," said Penelope. "And I know just what my speciality will be... watching from the audience!"

Hippo's Holiday

It was a warm, sunny morning in the jungle.

"A perfect time for a nice, long, relaxing holiday," thought Howard Hippo. "And there's nothing a hippo loves more than wallowing."

Wallowing in the river was Howard's favourite thing to do. He found a nice, cool, muddy spot and settled in. Howard had decided that on this holiday, he would wallow all the way to Hippo Hollow, a famous hippo holiday location. He was very excited about meeting new hippo friends there.

After three days of floating downstream, Howard arrived at Hippo Hollow. "It's even more beautiful than I imagined!" he exclaimed.

The next few days were the best of Howard's life. He had mud baths, made new hippo friends and splashed around in the cold water showers.

"I can't believe I haven't been on holiday here before," thought Howard.

And from that moment on, Howard went to Hippo Hollow on his holiday every year!

One Bear Lost

Ten sleepy bears wake from a winter's night.
One wanders out in the early morning light.
Nine scruffy bears wash in a sparkling stream.
One dries off, his fur all fresh and clean.

Eight hungry bears go on a hunt for food.
One wanders off when she smells something good!
Seven silent bears pad softly through the trees.
One sniffs some honey and goes looking for bees.
Six bears have fun in the snow.
One disappears – bottom high, head low.
Five strong bears climb up a slippery slope.
One slides down. She let go of the rope!

Four weary bears take a rest at the top.
One falls over, flippety-flop!
Three lively bears slide down the icy hill.
One stops to rest, calm and still.
Two brave bears paddle, steady and slow.
One gets stranded. Where should he go?
Nine weary bears have gone back home.
But look! One poor bear's left all alone.
One bear lost!
Nine worried bears call out for their friend.
Ten happy bears are back together again.
Ten tired bears are fast asleep in their cosy den.

My Hobby Horse

I had a little hobby horse, it was well shod,
It carried me to London, niddety nod,
And when we got to London we heard a great shout,
Down fell my hobby horse and I cried out:
"Up again, hobby horse, if thou be a beast,
When we get to our town we will have a feast,
And if there be but a little, why thou shall have some,
And dance to the bag-pipes and beating of the drum."

Engine, Engine

Engine, engine, number nine,
Sliding down Chicago line;
When she's polished she will shine,
Engine, engine, number nine.

Red Sky

Red sky at night,
Shepherd's delight;
Red sky in the morning,
Shepherd's warning.

Robin Hood

Robin Hood has gone to the wood;
He'll come back again if we are good.

There Was a Little Boy

There was a little boy and a little girl
Lived in an alley;
Says the little boy to the little girl,
"Shall I, oh, shall I?"
Says the little girl to the little boy,
"What shall we do?"
Says the little boy to the little girl,
"I will kiss you."

And That's All

There was an old man,
And he had a calf,
And that's half;
He took him out of the stall,
And put him on the wall,
And that's all.

The Mountain Mission

Jed was helping Elise the babysitter prepare dinner when Mum arrived home. She came into the kitchen, and put two plane tickets onto the table.

"Surprise! We're flying to Switzerland first thing tomorrow," she said. "So we'd better start packing!"

"Are we going skiing?" asked Jed excitedly.

"Yes, we're staying in a luxury ski resort," replied Mum.

"Wow!" said Elise. "I wish I was coming!"

Jed was curious. Why had his mum suddenly decided to take this holiday? It must have something to do with her work as a spy, he guessed.

While Mum was packing, Jed sneaked upstairs, turned on her computer and checked her emails.

He soon found out why they were really going. Some plans for a new spy plane had been stolen and Mum's mission was to get them back. An enemy agent called Max Blatt had the plans in his Swiss mountain hideout.

"This could be

Mum's most dangerous mission yet," Jed said to himself. "Good job I'm going along too."

"Wow!" said Jed, as they arrived in the ski resort. He almost forgot why they were really there as he looked up at the snow-covered mountains. He couldn't wait to get out on those ski runs. He loved skiing.

Mum was looking up, too. Jed followed her gaze. She was staring at a building at the top of a nearby mountain.

"That must be Blatt's hideout," Jed guessed. It was a long way up. Jed knew that his mum wasn't very good at skiing. She'd never make it all the way down that mountain. "I must act fast, before Mum tries anything stupid," he said to himself.

While Mum was unpacking, Jed went to explore the resort. Spotting a shop that sold fancy dress costumes, he had an idea. He took out the savings he'd brought with him, paid for a St Bernard dog costume and then smuggled it into his room.

"At least this silly disguise will keep me warm in the snow!" Jed thought as he put on the furry outfit the following morning.

There was only one way up the mountain, in the ski lift. Some skiers laughed when Jed got in.

"I didn't know dogs could ski!" one of them joked. At the top

of the mountain, Jed left the skiers behind. He made his way to the security fence surrounding Blatt's hideout and climbed over it.

Sneaking in through an open window, Jed found Blatt's office and began to look around for the plans. "They must be in here somewhere," he thought.

Suddenly three large dogs appeared. Jed was about to run when he saw that they didn't look at all fierce. They wanted to make friends.

"My costume must have fooled them," Jed thought with a relieved grin.

He found the plans, grabbed them and ran to the back door, almost tripping over a dog basket. "That will come in handy!" he said, picking it up. It was great fun sledging

down the mountain in the basket.

Soon Jed was back in his hotel. He went up to the reception desk.

"Will you send these papers up to Frances Best in Room 303, please?" he asked, handing over the plans.

"Mum will love the room service in this hotel!" Jed chuckled to himself.

The Work of Art

Eddie had a bright idea. "Let's put a notice on the school noticeboard," he said. *Eddie and Josh's Odd Job Service – No job too big or too small.*

"Let's do it!" said Josh.

On Friday afternoon, Miss Price, the headteacher of the nursery next door, called the boys into her office. "I've seen your notice," she told them. "I have a job for you: I'd like you to paint the nursery playground wall."

"When shall we start?" asked Josh.

"Tomorrow after school," said Miss Price.

After school the next day, the caretaker carried some paint pots and paintbrushes into the playground.

"Miss Price didn't say what colour she wanted the wall to be painted," the caretaker said, opening the pots of paint. "I'll leave you to choose." Then he went back into his shed at the side of the playground.

Eddie and Josh looked at the paints. There was red, yellow, green and purple paint.

"We should use all the colours to paint a huge picture," said Eddie.

Josh nodded. "Let's paint some footballers," he suggested, picking up a pot of green paint.

"No, some monsters," said Eddie, taking a pot of purple paint.

"Footballers!" said Josh.

"Monsters!" argued Eddie. He flicked some purple paint at the wall.

"Footballers!" yelled Josh, flicking some green paint over Eddie's purple paint.

By the time Josh and Eddie had finished arguing, the whole wall was splattered with purple and green, and there wasn't a monster or a footballer in sight.

"Oh dear!" said Josh, staring at the wall.

They left the paints and hurried off home.

First thing on Monday morning, Josh and Eddie were called in to see Miss Price.

Miss Price was quiet for a moment. Then she clapped her hands in delight. "Well done!" she said. "What a fantastic piece of modern art!"

Eddie and Josh grinned at each other as Miss Price handed them an envelope.

"Here's your money for a job well done!" she said.

Hide-and-seek

It was playtime at school. The animals were playing hide-and-seek. Lucy Lion counted to ten. The animals ran to hide.

"Ninety-nine... One hundred! I'm coming!" called Lucy.

Lucy looked high and low. She couldn't find Helga Hippo. Lucy looked high and low. She couldn't find Mikey Monkey. Lucy looked high and low. She couldn't find Jed Giraffe.

"Where is everybody?" Lucy wondered. She kept looking. She looked and looked and looked until she started to get tired.

When the bell rang for the end of playtime the animals came out of their hiding places.

"Where's Lucy?" asked Mrs Beak, the teacher.

They looked high and low for Lucy. Helga Hippo couldn't find her. Mikey Monkey couldn't find her. Jed Giraffe couldn't find her.

Then Mrs Beak found her. Lucy had given up. She was fast asleep under a tree!

Smasher Can

Dozer was busy moving sand. Digger was busy scooping. Dumper was busy tipping. They were building a house.

Fred the builder was fixing the roof. He had climbed up there using a ladder.

"Look out!" said Digger.

"Look out!" said Dozer.

Dumper wasn't looking where he was going. He bumped into the ladder. *Crash!* The ladder fell down.

"Help!" said Fred. He was stuck on the roof.

"I can't reach," said Dumper.

"I can't reach," said Digger.

"I can't reach, either," said Dozer.

"I know who can reach," said Dumper. "Smasher can!" Smasher was a crane.

Very carefully, Smasher swung his big metal ball towards Fred. Fred climbed onto it.

Then Smasher lowered the ball down to the ground.

"Thanks, Smasher!" grinned Fred, putting his ladder back up.

"Sorry, Fred," said Dumper. "I'll look where I'm going next time."

Ducks' Ditty

All along the backwater,
Through the rushes tall,
Ducks are a-dabbling,
Up tails all!

Ducks' tails, drakes' tails,
Yellow feet a-quiver,
Yellow bills all out of sight
Busy in the river!

Slushy green undergrowth
Where the roach swim
Here we keep our larder,
Cool and full and dim.

Every one for what he likes!
We like to be
Heads down, tails up,
Dabbling free!

High in the blue above
Swifts whirl and call;
We are down a-dabbling,
Up tails all!

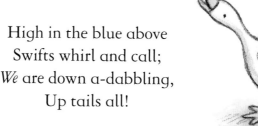

The Kangaroo

Old Jumpety-Bumpety-Hop-and-Go-One
Was lying asleep on his side in the sun.
This old kangaroo, he was whisking the flies
(With his long glossy tail) from his ears and his eyes.
Jumpety-Bumpety-Hop-and-Go-One
Was lying asleep on his side in the sun,
Jumpety-Bumpety-Hop!

I Just Can't Sleep

It's time to sleep.
I've brushed my teeth
And read my book,
I've put my bathrobe
On the hook, and...
I just can't sleep.
The bed's too hot,
The light's too bright,
There are far too many
Sounds tonight, and...
Maybe I'll sleep.
I think I might,
I think I'll – yawn –
Turn out the light.
Good night.
Zzzzzz...

Holiday Time

We're off on holiday. Oh, what fun!
There may be rain or there may be sun.
But we'll all have a lovely time together,
And enjoy ourselves, whatever the weather!

Crazy Animals

Stomp! Stomp! Zebra's proud,
Because he stands out in a crowd.

Squeak! Squeak! Little Mouse
Scampers quickly through the house.

Roar! Roar! Hear Lion roar!
Eats his lunch and still wants more!

Miaow! Miaow! Have you seen
Naughty Kitty licking cream?

Bark! Bark! Messy Pup!
Hides his bone, then digs it up.

Baa! Baa! Clever Sheep!
Counting lambs to fall asleep.

Elephant's Trunk

Elephant loves to blow his trunk
At the start of every day.
"Tarrantarra!" he loudly trumps,
To wake his friends to play.

Elephant's trunk is useful
To shower and to squirt.
Down at the pool his friends join in,
To wash off all the dirt.

And when it comes to mealtimes,
A trunk can help once more –
To reach the highest, juiciest leaves
That jungle friends adore.

But best of all for Elephant,
When his friends are tucked up snug,
He loves to wrap his trunk around,
And give them a big hug!

Lost and Found

It was Show and Tell time in Class 2B.

Sam and Jed showed their new Perry Hill football shirts.

"Who else is a Perry Hill fan?" asked Miss Bell.

Joe put up his hand. So did Clare, the new girl in class.

Joe sighed. He really wanted to go and see Perry Hill play that Saturday, but it cost five pounds and he didn't have any pocket money left.

That break, Joe was kicking a ball around on his own when he saw something fluttering by. Joe leapt and grabbed it. It was a five pound note. He put the money in his pocket. Result!

After break, though, Clare was very upset.

"I've lost five pounds," she said to Miss Bell.

Joe thought about it.

He knew that the money was Clare's. Deep down, he had known all along that it wasn't his.

"I found it," said Joe.

"Thank you!" said Clare.

"Well done, Joe!" said Miss Bell.

The next day after school, Joe

spotted Jared Jones at the school gate. He was the top striker at Perry Hill football club.

"Look!" said Joe to Sam and Jed. "Jared Jones! I wonder what he's doing here?"

"He's talking to Clare!" said Sam.

"Why isn't he talking to us?" said Jed. "We're much better at football than she is."

Then Clare called across the playground, "Over here, Joe!"

Joe went across the playground towards Jared. He felt a bit nervous about meeting him. Jared was such an amazing footballer! Joe really hoped that one day he would be as good as Jared was.

"Jared is my big brother," Clare told Joe.

"Wow!" said Joe.

"Thanks for helping my sister," said Jared, handing Joe a ticket. Joe looked. It was three tickets to Saturday's match, in the best seats in the stadium.

"See you at the match on Saturday," said Jared. "And I hope you and your friends can come and meet the rest of the Perry Hill team after the match as well."

"Thanks!" said Joe.

Tickly Sheep

One morning, Farmer Fred was in the kitchen having his hair cut. Farmer Fred's wife Jenny was snipping away with the scissors.

"Hurry up," said Farmer Fred. "I've got to shear all the sheep today."

"Well, stop wriggling," laughed Jenny.

"But it tickles," chuckled Farmer Fred.

"I've never known anyone make such a fuss about having their hair cut," laughed Jenny, making the final snip.

Farmer Fred and Patch went up to Fern Hill to round up the sheep. Farmer Fred whistled a signal to Patch: Peep! Peeeep! Patch ran around the field, herding the sheep towards the yard.

Farmer Fred whistled a different signal: Peeeep! Peep! Patch soon had the sheep lined up outside the barn.

Inside the barn, Farmer Fred switched on his shears. Whizz, whizz, whizz went the shears.

"There's nothing quite like shearing sheep," he smiled, and began to sing.

One by one, Farmer Fred sheared the sheep. The woolly fleeces which came off the sheep collected on the barn floor. All went well until it was Shirley Sheep's turn.

Whizz, whizz, went the shears. As soon as the buzzing shears touched her side, Shirley began to wriggle and jiggle.

"Stop wriggling," cried Farmer Fred, as he tried to hold her still. He had forgotten just how ticklish Shirley was!

"Rumbling radishes!" Fred gasped, when he had finished. Shirley had wriggled about so much that she had big bald patches all over her woolly fleece. She looked very peculiar!

"Never fear, I've an idea!" cried Farmer Fred cheerfully. He dashed off to his workshop and disappeared inside.

Very soon, Farmer Fred came out of the workshop holding two old tyres tied onto some rope.

"This," Farmer Fred said grandly, "is my Super Sheep-defleecer!"

Farmer Fred helped Shirley Sheep to step through the tyres and slowly lifted her off the ground. He turned on the shears and tried again.

And although Shirley wriggled and giggled, Farmer Fred
sheared off all her wool.

Farmer Fred let Shirley Sheep down and helped her from
the tyres.

"Baa?" asked Shirley Sheep. She looked at the other
animals. But they were all laughing so much at Shirley Sheep's
stripy haircut they couldn't answer.

While Fred collected up the sheep fleeces, the animals
gathered around Shirley Sheep.

"She can't possibly go around looking like that," said Hetty
Hen. "Everyone will laugh at her."

"We have to do something," agreed Harry Horse. "Patch,
what can we do?"

Suddenly Patch remembered Farmer Fred having his
hair cut.

"Woof, woof!" he barked. "Leave it to me." Patch raced to
the kitchen where Jenny had put the scissors, comb and mirror
into a bowl.

"Woof, woof!" barked Patch, pushing the bowl outside just as Farmer Fred was crossing the yard.

"What's that, Patch?" laughed Fred. "I haven't got time to give you a hair cut now." Just then Shirley trotted up.

"Hold on!" said Farmer Fred. "I've had an even better idea!" He picked up the bowl and raced back to the barn.

Before long Shirley was sitting in her very own wool-cutting parlour.

"Now, would madam like a short and curly cut?" laughed Farmer Fred, as he began snipping away.

And this time, Shirley didn't giggle or wriggle until all that was left was a curly fringe.

"Perfect," said Farmer Fred, as he tied a huge blue ribbon in Shirley's lovely curls.

Shirley walked proudly around the farmyard. Everyone, including Jenny, gathered around to admire her.

They all agreed that she was the prettiest sheep on the farm.

"I've never known anyone make such a fuss about having their hair cut," said Farmer Fred. Jenny looked at Patch and laughed.

Hot Cross Buns

Hot cross buns!
Hot cross buns!
One-a-penny, two-a-penny,
Hot cross buns!
If you have no daughters,
Give them to your sons,
One-a-penny, two-a-penny,
Hot cross buns!

Wash Hands

Wash, hands, wash,
Daddy's gone to plough;
If you want your hands wash'd,
Have them wash'd now.

Willie Wastle

I, Willie Wastle,
Stand on my castle,
An' a' the dogs o' your toon,
Will no' drive Willie Wastle down.

Richard Dick

Richard Dick upon a stick,
Sampson on a sow,
We'll ride away to Colley fair
To buy a horse to plough.

Parliament Soldiers

High diddle ding, did you hear the bells ring?
The parliament soldiers are gone to the king.
Some they did laugh, and some they did cry,
To see the parliament soldiers go by.

Oats and Beans

Oats and beans and barley grow,
Oats and beans and barley grow,
Do you or I or anyone know,
How oats and beans and barley grow?

First the farmer sows his seeds,
Then he stands and takes his ease,
Stamps his feet and claps his hands,
Turns around to view the land.

Fat Cat

Eddie and Josh had set up a pet-sitting service. Their first job was to feed Fluffy, Mr and Mrs Cole's cat, while they went on holiday for a week.

"Don't forget, Fluffy needs feeding three times a day," Mrs Cole told the boys, as she handed over the huge cat.

When Mrs Cole was in the car, Mr Cole turned to Eddie and Josh. "Try not to let Fluffy eat too much!" he whispered. "See you next week."

"Mr Cole is right," said Josh a week later, as he and Eddie watched Fluffy tuck into her twenty-first bowl of food. "Fluffy definitely eats too much."

"Let's see if I can stop her," said Eddie. He made a barking noise, like a dog.

Eddie and Josh had never seen a cat move so fast. She bolted through the cat flap into the back garden and up the nearest tree.

Josh and Eddie ran outside.

"Here, Fluffy!" Josh called. But Fluffy wouldn't come down.

"Now look what you've done, Eddie!" said Josh.

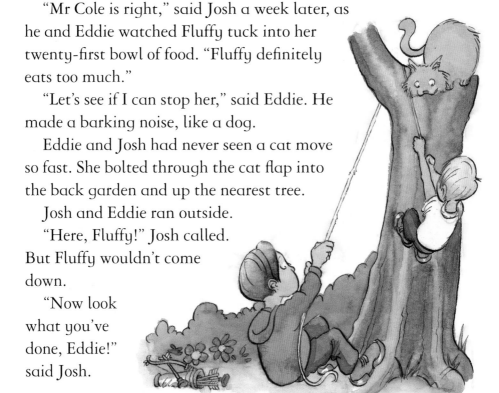

"Don't panic, I'll get her down," said Eddie. He went home to fetch his toy bow and arrow and a rope. Then he tied the rope to one of the arrows and fired it over a branch.

"Hold one end of the rope, Josh," Eddie said. Slowly, Eddie pulled himself up the tree using the rope. "Phew! This is hard work!" he panted.

But just as Eddie reached the branch that Fluffy sat on, the cat scampered back down the tree trunk all by herself.

Eddie looked down. "Oh no!" he cried. "I'm stuck now!"

"It looks like we arrived home just in time!" said Mr Cole, walking into the garden. He put a stepladder against the tree and helped Eddie down. "What were you doing up there?" he asked.

Eddie and Josh explained, and Mr Cole laughed.

When Mrs Cole came outside she didn't find it quite so funny. "Fluffy doesn't usually climb trees," she said, cuddling the enormous cat and frowning at Eddie and Josh.

Fluffy purred and looked smug.

Naughty Duckling

Mummy Duck is in a flap.
"My naughty duckling won't come back!"

She's off to chase him, on his tail –
Following Little Duckling's trail.

"Go over the hill!" the little foal neighs,
"I saw Little Duckling run that way!"

"Along the fence!" baby calf moos,
"You'll catch him if you hurry, too!"

The piglets oink, "We saw him slide!
Up on the roof and down the side!"

"Look under here!" the lambs all baa,
"He can't have gone so very far!"

"He came past here!" cheeps little chick,
"He said hello, then ran off, quick!"

And there he is! He loves to roam.
But most of all he loves his home!

I Wish...

I wish I was an elephant,
'Cause it would make me laugh.
To use my nose like a garden hose
To rinse myself in the bath.

I wish I was a chameleon,
Chameleons are best.
I'd change my colour and life would be fuller,
For a change is as good as a rest.

I wish I was a dolphin,
A dolphin would be my wish.
Leaping and splashing, I'd be very dashing,
And swim along with the fish.

I wish I was an ostrich,
An ostrich would be grand.
But if I got scared, would I be prepared
To bury my head in the sand?

I wish I had more wishes,
But now my game is through,
I'm happy to be quite simply me,
Enjoying a day at the zoo.

Two Little Dickie Birds

Two little dickie birds sitting on a wall,
One named Peter, one named Paul.
Fly away, Peter!
Fly away, Paul!
Come back, Peter!
Come back, Paul!

Once I Saw a Little Bird

Once I saw a little bird
Come hop, hop, hop,
So I cried, "Little bird,
Will you stop, stop, stop?"
And was going to the window,
To say, "How do you do?"
But he shook his little tail,
And far away he flew.

Little Robin Redbreast

Little Robin Redbreast
Sat upon a rail:
Niddle-noddle went his head!
Wiggle-waggle went his tail.

Intery, Mintery, Cutery, Corn

Intery, mintery, cutery, corn,
Apple seed and apple thorn.
Wire, briar, limber, lock,
Three geese in a flock.

One flew east and one flew west;
One flew over the cuckoo's nest.

The North Wind Doth Blow

The north wind doth blow,
And we shall have snow,
And what will poor Robin do then?
Poor thing!

He'll sit in a barn,
And to keep himself warm,
Will hide his head under his wing.
Poor thing!

Magpies

One for sorrow, two for joy,
Three for a girl, four for a boy,
Five for silver, six for gold,
Seven for a secret never to be told.

Pet Prize

It was school fair day. There was going to be a Best Pet Competition.

Tom's friends all brought their pets. Sammy had a hamster. Carlos had a ginger cat. Deepak had his rabbit, Sooty.

"I wish I had a pet," said Tom. Miss Bell was going to judge the competition. Her dog Chip had come too.

Chip was small and brown and had a very waggy tail.

"Can I pat him?" asked Tom.

"Yes," said Miss Bell. "He's very friendly."

Tom patted Chip. Chip wagged his tail furiously.

"I wish I had a pet like you," whispered Tom to Chip.

Chip barked understandingly.

Miss Bell looked at the pets.

She looked at a rabbit, two hamsters, four gerbils, one cat, three mice, two dogs…

"And the prize for best-groomed pet goes to… Carlos!" she said, giving him a medal.

Sammy won the prize for friendliest pet.

Deepak won the prize for most well-behaved pet.

Tom wished more and more that he had a pet of his own to enter in the competition.

Then Miss Bell looked around. "Where is Chip?" she asked. Chip was missing!

"We must find him!" said Miss Bell. She was very worried.

"I'll go and look for him," said Tom.

He looked at the book stall. Chip wasn't there.

He looked at the raffle stall. Chip wasn't there either.

Then Tom saw a wagging tail. He looked under the cake stall – and there was Chip, licking up the crumbs!

Chip wagged his tail when he saw Tom and barked.

"Time to go back," said Tom.

At the end of the competition, Miss Bell gave out a special prize.

"And this prize is for Best Pet Finder," she said with a smile. "The winner is... Tom!"

Index

383